THAT TIME
IN
MALOMBA

THAT TIME IN MALOMBA

JAMES HAMILTON-PATERSON

Soho Press, Inc.
1 Union Square
New York, N.Y. 10003

First published in the U.K. by Hutchinson in 1990
under the title *The Bell-Boy*

Library of Congress Cataloging-in-Publication Data

Hamilton-Paterson, James.
That Time in Malomba / James Hamilton-Paterson.
p.   cm.
ISBN 0-939149-42-7
I. Title.
PR6058.A5543T47   1990
823'.914—dc20   90-9976
                                                        CIP

Manufactured in the United States of America

For Hazel Worthy

THAT TIME
IN
MALOMBA

Waking beneath the vine, Laki would leave his hutch on the roof and go out into the turquoise dawn. Standing among litter (pails, washing-lines, pigeon shit) he could look over town to the surrounding hills of coconut and bamboo whose western slopes slept darkly even as their sunward faces blazed. In the middle ground a profusion of temples of one sort or another, fierce canonical pressures beneath Malomba's surface having caused religious buildings to bubble and mould themselves freakishly like cooling glass-ware. From them arose competing sounds of clergy per-forming their various rites to celebrate daybreak. The mosque's glass pencil had already spoken; the weed-tufted skull of the pro-cathedral still dozed. A bronze trumpet blew over one quarter and from another came the distant thrashing of gongs.

Meanwhile the pigeons which had passed the night in their end of Laki's loft would be circling the sky with a clapping of wings. Now and again amid all this matin din could be heard the noise of water falling four storeys on to a sheet of corrugated iron lying among the weeds below, an awning which had long ago slipped from above one of the Hotel Nirvana's windows. The water came through a cement spout slimy from laundry. The tap feeding it had lost its handle to a brass thief and the stump of its valve was held down by rubber cut from an inner tube. At this hour of day – before secular Malomba was properly awake and when the town's women had not yet begun their washing –

1

water pressure was high and spurted fine jets between the bindings.

Squatting at the tap Laki rinsed himself, using a sliver of detergent soap saved in a coconut shell which he afterwards lodged among the gourds festooning his loft. This den on the hotel's roof was the most prized thing in his life. Made largely of mud bricks, it had originally been designed as a spacious pigeon loft, one pierced and battlemented wall remaining of an intricate city of cells and perches and roosts. Over the years the interests of the proprietor in pigeons as a source of income had waned and increased and waned again and in the meantime the loft had decayed, been patched together, grown derelict once more. A vine had taken root low down in one wall and had grown inwards, where its dense tanglings now effectively divided the cell before bursting out through a hole in the ceiling which admitted sun, rain, pigeons. On one side of this vine the birds lived and cooed and on the other Laki had his domain. When he had first been given the exclusive use of the place it was with the indifferent magnanimity which awards a dog a leaky packing-case as kennel. Over the three years of his apprenticeship he had scrounged and patched so that sheets of tin and coconut thatch now kept out the worst of the weather and prevented the walls' further dissolution. He had found a door and stolen a padlock. Now at night he stretched in luxury on his reed pallet, a luxury scarcely known in the town's slums below where families slept jammed together on the floor of a single room.

He had once thought of clearing out the vine, thereby increasing his space and making it possible to mend the roof above it, but he had grown fond of the shrub. The shifting dapples of sunlight filtering through its leaves pleased him, and in any case it effectively segregated him from the birds. Now and again he puzzled as to where it obtained its nourishment: the mud bricks at the base of its stem seemed hardly enough. Maybe over the years the roots had worked their way into the hotel's roof and down inside its walls right to the earth four storeys beneath? Certainly the ceilings of the top-floor rooms were cracked and leaky. No. 41 in particular was only ever assigned to the most derelict foreigners or travelling salesmen. It lay directly under the laundry area and suds often gathered on its floor.

Another reason for keeping the vine was its usefulness as a wardrobe. On one of its many arms Laki now hung his towel and from a wire coathanger elsewhere took a white cotton uniform. Propped in a woody elbow was a triangle of broken mirror from Room 41. Standing before it he slicked his hair with a wet fragment of comb. It was black and luxuriant and made a satisfying wave which gleamed in the early sunlight streaming in above. He peered forward and examined his chin. He wished he needed a shave, but it was pointless to pretend this was any more necessary today than it had been yesterday. 'Anything can happen at your age,' Raju the night porter would say encouragingly. 'Even overnight. Some boys are like plants. The sap rises with hardly a sign of a bud, then suddenly one morning they're in flower. Just like that.' Laki lived in daily expectation of a beard, not being sure of anything much, not even of his age. He thought he might be getting on for fifteen; his mother had always been vague.

❦

There arrived in town this very morning the Hemony family, more than usually dishevelled after a battering night in the overnight bus from the capital. Dawn had found them still up among the jungled hills, Jason asleep with his head in his mother's lap, his sister Zoe curled up on the seat behind. The sun which was lighting up the eastern summits for Laki on his rooftop was not yet high enough to spill its generous

3

fire into their road which lay in deep shades of grey between walls of trunks. The rubber, coconuts, candelabrums, mock-quassias, gibbet-trees which had accompanied them into last night were emerging once more, faithfully unchanged. They looked identical in every respect. Only the numbed impression of episodes from the previous nine hours – a puncture, three stops in provincial bus stations where brutal fluorescent glare had woken the passengers – convinced Tessa that they had indeed been covering distance. Otherwise they might just as well have been riding a piece of elaborate machinery designed as a film prop to suggest a harsh journey: endlessly repeating scenery and the pounding of iron chassis and wood seats over ruts.

'Not striving, not grasping, I am in bliss,' she said to herself out of habit. Her back ached and at dawns like this she was increasingly prey to heretical notions, such as that now and again her life felt like one aimless bus journey. To look back was pointless, of course, since there was only *now*. Had she done so, the history of her two children and their ponytailed father's defection might have blurred into a wearying sense of seeming always to have been on a potholed road with trouble around the next bend. Exactly twenty years ago she had joined a party in a decrepit Dormobile to Kathmandu. Passports, body searches, desperate cables for funds, shot through with heady freedoms and the smell of stale clothing.

It had begun there but not exactly then. Tessa could never have been present at her own point of departure; she was in pigtails at an English private school when Ken Kesey and his Merry Pranksters boarded a psychedelic bus and began their magic acid trip round America. Each turn of its wheels had shed religions in a glittering dust which settled over the landscape of the next decade. But soon she and her peers had driven off through that dust in their own buses and minivans to the weirdest places. Twenty years on, the flower children wore suits and those same places had been

4

thoroughly unweirded by the duty-free set since it was now far cheaper to fly. What exactly was it, then, which still locked her into this penitential form of travel? Not poverty, at any rate. Dogged constancy, maybe.

The sun had come up and suddenly they were at the edge of hills in whose hollow Malomba lay. The passengers left off dozing and began running their hands through their hair, yawning, dabbing their mouths with clean folded handkerchiefs. They were driving directly into morning, the brilliance pouring through the cracked green-tinted wind-screen past the dangling talismans and eclipsing the red bulb in the shrine nodding on its spring. This violent clap of light brought the children upright, rubbing their eyes.

'This it?' asked Jason. '*Madonna*, what a dump.' The outskirts with their vulcanising shops and soft drink depots led to honking streets clotted with people and donkeys and motor-tricycles. 'What are we doing here?'

'I told you, Jay. This is where the psychic surgeons are.'

'I don't see any.'

A road whose width was reduced by booths jammed end to end and laden with bolts of material. Other stalls were piled with aluminium and plastic ware or hung with paper-chains of lottery tickets. From them loudspeakers blared the conflicting claims of salesmen. The bus bumped over a mush of sugarcane stalks and coconut husks and they were in the terminus. The passengers stood up and thronged the gangway, shouldering zipper bags decorated with the decals of non-existent airlines. Past them and against their grain came pushing a boy in flimsy uniform.

'Yes, missus. Yes, missus. What hotel?'

'I beg your pardon?' Tessa's spine as she stood up sent brilliant electric bolts down the back of both legs. Suddenly she wished they hadn't come. These wearisome touts . . . The boy was impervious.

'Yes, missus. Hotel. What name you have?'

She found a scrap of paper in her Tibetan wool bag.

'We're already booked, thank you. The Golden Fortune Hotel. I'm sorry.'

'Golden Fortune? Chinese hotel, Golden Fortune. Very bad hotel. Very dirty. Finish now.'

'What do you mean?'

'Finish. No more. Big fire one week ago. Come, I show you.'

'Terrific,' said Jason. 'A great bit of booking.'

'How was I to know?'

'He's probably lying,' said Zoe. 'We'll find it ourselves. What's the address?'

'All finish,' the boy repeated. 'I take you to hotel, more cheap, more clean.' And then the clincher. 'Very near.'

'How near?' Tessa wanted to know. She was not yet sure of being able to walk at all.

'Two minutes, maybe four.'

'What's it called?'

But he was propelling them gently out into the light and din like tousled sleepwalkers.

'It'll be shitty,' said Jason. 'It'll be like the last place. I'll wind up having to sleep with her again.'

'Actually, I'd rather have a floor with cockroaches than share with a smelly twelve-year-old.'

'Oh, do stop it, you two.' Tessa was in anguish and when their young guide looked up at her seriously and put his hand over hers she broke the habit of a travelling lifetime and found herself surrendering her bag. Pain; a glance; an expression of the eyes, she thought passively. Just then a scarlet jeep with a shiny white plastic hood glided alongside them. In the general hubbub it made no sound and she turned her head to see four men in sports shirts and mirror sunglasses staring back. It went past and became lost to view but for a moment she retained the memory of sun flaring off its chrome bumpers and dancing across the hood's tautness as it trembled to the motor; that and the tip of its long aerial switching above the traffic like the tail of a beast of prey. Suddenly she noticed the boy was no longer with them.

'That's funny, where's he gone?'

'He's got our *bag*, Mum. It's not funny at all. What have you done? Little bugger. Some urchin comes up to you and you give him all our stuff?' Zoe was nearly in tears. 'He hasn't got the money too, has he? You're *joking*. And our passports? Jesus, Mum, it's not your back that needs mumbo-jumbo surgery, but your head. Well, *you* get us to the police station and *you* do the explaining.'

But just at this moment – which had made for itself a horrid island in the middle of the pavement round which curious people flowed – and just as they were being hailed from ankle level by a beaming legless vendor of sunglasses, the boy reappeared with the bag.

'We lost you,' said Tessa in relief. She wanted to cry.

'Short cut only.' He smiled encouragingly as if he knew to the last adrenal pang what had been thought. 'Very near now.' And to her surprise they turned a corner and there was a hotel with a tangled bush on its roof. The walk from the bus station, including that dreadful timeless moment, had taken them precisely four minutes as he had said.

'That's it?' asked Zoe. 'Hotel Nirvana?'

'Nirbana, yes. I am to working here, living here.'

Behind the Reception desk the board of numbered hooks was hung almost gaplessly with keys, scarcely a sight to cheer a hotel proprietor first thing in the morning. Raju had gone off duty and it was Mr Muffy himself who stood behind the counter, gloomily testing a Japanese adding-up machine which he had just bought from some Indian sharpers in the Wednesday Market. Mr Muffy had a long-standing difficulty with sums. He already had an old pocket calculator whose black window lit up with oblique red figures, but the phrase 'business efficiency' was in the air. His new machine did nothing to make his accounts more palatable, however. Indeed, he had just decided he preferred the calculator since its grim news could be made to vanish into thin air at the touch of a switch, whereas this new machine printed everything out on expensive little rolls of paper.

On seeing the Hemonys he summoned up a smile of welcome, while studiedly ignoring Laki's proud grin at having captured some early trade. Vain monkey that he was, what did he think he was being paid for? *And* given board and a luxurious free apartment?

'Good morning, good morning,' said Mr Muffy. 'You are from?'

'Oh, England I suppose,' said Tessa. 'The capital,' said Zoe. 'The bus,' said Jason. They all spoke simultaneously in the lacklustre tones common to new arrivals in Malomba, there being no restful way of reaching the town. 'We'd like a room,' went on Tessa. 'Three rooms,' said Zoe.

'Passports, please.' He was suddenly businesslike. Three rooms. Only last week Laki had dragged home an American woman who turned out to have wanted no more than breakfast. The insolent child had had the effrontery to demand his commission, too, which earned him a stinging ear. Still, Mr Muffy wasn't holding out much hope for these new arrivals. Like most Malombans he fancied himself a practised judge of foreigners' wealth, and like most Malombans got it wrong much of the time. He and his countrymen were easily misled by people who dressed down; his culture insisted that wealth should be displayed or faked, never concealed. Nonetheless, behind him lay long years of experience in running the Nirvana and he had learned to intuit subtler signs of tourist indigence. He was under few illusions about his hotel. No matter how good Laki's touting was – and he was prepared to concede nothing – the better-heeled foreigners tended to put up elsewhere at places like the Golden Fortune. A well-named establishment, reflected Mr Muffy bitterly. A fortune was exactly what they were making, those damned Chinese.

Miserly and clannish, they were ruining this country. They simply moved in, and before you knew where you were the honest local was being squeezed out by unscrupulous monopolists. Them and the Indians . . . He flicked through the tattered passports Tessa had laid on the counter. 'You are Italian?'

'No, look – these are British passports. We are Italian *residents*.'

'Dual nationality,' said Mr Muffy wisely. 'Very useful.'

'It's not dual at all. We're English people who happen to be living in Italy.'

'So you are from Italy? We have to be accurate. The police here are very strict for your protection. These forms must be filled in truthfully.' He pushed three registration blanks towards her which looked as if they had been run off on scrap paper. Here and there the print was so faint as to be illegible. His finger found the phrase *Country of Origin*.

'We're not actually *from* Italy. Actually.'

'May I see your air ticket please, madam?' Tessa rummaged in her bag and produced it. Not striving, not grasping, she told herself inwardly. 'Exactly. You are from Rome. Rome is the capital of Italy, is it not?'

When the forms had been filled in to Mr Muffy's liking, she asked, 'How much are your rooms?'

'We have an excellent room for three at a hundred and sixty-five a night. Very beautiful view of Malomba. Glass Minaret, Temple of Ashes, everything.'

'Three singles,' said Zoe firmly. 'For a hundred and forty in all.'

'*In all?* Not possible, I regret.'

'Then we're off. Come on, Mum. We can try that place we saw on the way.'

'One hundred and fifty,' agreed Mr Muffy with affected resignation. 'Fifty each, without breakfast.'

'With.'

This one was the brains of the family, he thought to

9

himself, looking at her passport again. Only fifteen, and already such a self-possessed young lady. His attitude became flavoured with the mixture of gallantry and lust which might inform any man dealing with a nubile girl with long blonde hair and a sullen mouth. Put her on a separate floor. 'You drive a hard bargain, miss.' She stared back at him impassively, however, so with a proprietorial gesture he scooped three keys off the rack and thrust them at Laki. He took some pleasure in assigning the son to No. 41.

The Nirvana Hotel had no lift. The main staircase began with a certain faded grandeur, having white marble steps which before the steep rise in the price of brass had been carpeted with a maroon drugget held in place by gleaming stair-rods. Now only the holes for the fittings remained. Once round the half-landing the marble ran out suddenly and gave way to cement. Laki, bringing up the rear with their bags, called cheerfully, 'How long you stay?'

'We don't know yet,' said Tessa. 'Malomba's an important spiritual place, isn't it? There'll be a lot to see.'

'Oh, very much to seeing here,' his voice came up behind her. 'Malomba have thirty-nine temples, churches, moskies. The Glass . . . '

'What about the healers?' Zoe wanted to know. 'This *is* the right place for psychic surgery, isn't it?'

'Yes, miss. Psychic surgeons we have. Very famous, very good men. You like? I know all of them. If you want I show. Special price because I am friend.'

'We already have an introduction, thank you,' Tessa told him from up ahead. 'A gentleman named Tapranne.'

'You to knowing *hadlam* Tapranne?' Laki's tone was of surprise and respect. All Malombans knew he was the best healer in town and therefore in the entire country. Assuredly most of the other surgeons, if not actual charlatans, were in it for the money. When *hadlam* Tapranne operated, however, money was never discussed. Even if he cured you completely no fee was asked or expected. Laki assumed he

10

must be immensely rich because his patients were so grateful their generosity knew no bounds. Last year a famous Indian film star had come all the way from Delhi to see him. The man had been suffering from a malignancy which made movement agonising and he flew out his specially padded Rolls Royce so he could make his visit in comfort. After only one session with *hadlam* Tapranne he was completely cured. The *hadlam* had removed a black tumour the size of a pomegranate from near his spine. There were pictures of it in the next day's press and ordinary doctors had declared it a miracle. There and then the Indian had given the *hadlam* his Rolls Royce and had walked all the way back to the capital. That had been the real proof that something unique had occurred: an Indian film star *walking*. It had taken him a fortnight and when he arrived he described himself as a 'changed man'. In consequence of this and other miracles, people were coming from all over the world to consult Tapranne and he was by no means easy to see. If these Hemonys had access to him, they must be richer and better-connected than they looked.

'We don't yet know him personally but we shall be seeing him in a week or so,' Tessa was saying. 'How much further?'

'Here, my lady.' Laki juggled with the keys and opened a door in a dim passage. 'This is my lady's room. Special view of Redemptorist Fathers.'

The room was exactly what everybody expected. They had all climbed many identical staircases before and seen rooms with a gnawed gap between floorboards and wainscoting, a cement bathroom with single tap and no shower-head, a seatless lavatory bowl. Two mosquito nets of grubby nylon holed by insomniacs' cigarettes hung from the ceiling, tucked loosely into their hoops. The beds beneath them were made up with clean unironed sheets with the word 'Nirvana' printed on them in washed-out blue.

'Look at view, my lady.'

Tessa crossed to the window and was agreeably surprised to find herself looking into a tropical garden of great luxuriance. Between palms and mangoes the grass was cropped by wandering deer. Among the dapples of sunlight blossoms glowed. A magnificent cloud-tree floated its breezy sacks of opalescent bloom above a pavilion in the form of a miniature stone pagoda reached by a tiny hump of bridge over a stream. From this garden a scent of flowers poured in through the glassless window-frame.

'Oh, it's lovely,' she said. 'Do come and look at this, you two.'

'This room suits my lady?'

'It's perfect.'

'I to showing the other rooms. Come,' he said to Zoe and Jason.

'You've been very kind and helpful,' Tessa thanked him. 'What's your name?'

'Laki, my lady.'

'Lucky?' She studied him and then said earnestly, 'Yes, you are. I feel it. And so are we to have met you, although of course it was *meant*. What happiness! I am in bliss.'

Her children followed their guide and tramped dourly upstairs.

Zoe surveyed her darkened room impassively. 'It'll do. At least I've got it to myself.'

'Only please to keeping shutters closed, miss. So plenty air come in but no monkeys.'

'Monkeys?'

'Oh, yes, miss, many monkeys here in Malomba. Living in jungle and coming down for eating in early morning. Also living in Redemptorist Fathers because many trees. Stealing, stealing everything. And biting. To being careful, miss.'

She threw open the shutters. This room was at one side of the hotel and gave over the flat cement roof of the Bank of the Divine Lotus next door. Beneath an awning of fronds

12

jury-rigged on bamboo poles she could see chickens penned in. Some rusted filing-cabinet drawers served as nesting boxes and were stuffed with hay. Leaning out and looking towards the hotel's rear, she could see an edge of the massive greenery her mother's room overlooked.

'Well, thank you, Lucky. I'll come and see yours later,' she added to her brother.

Room 41 was at its celebrated best. The laundrywomen on the roof overhead were busy. Water dripped into the shower stall from a black wound in the ceiling whose lips were mottled with moulds; at one end of this crack depended a tuft of green beard glistening with slime. Chatter came down with narrow clarity as through a cardboard tube, then a scraping as an aluminium washing bowl was upended. The dripping increased momentarily, became a stream of cloudy rinse-water, ebbed again.

This room faced the street, but being only one floor lower than Laki's pigeon-loft its view over Malomba was scarcely less panoramic. The Nirvana was built on a gentle slope which marked the beginning of the hills, and when new had stood peacefully apart from the rest of the little town in its own garden. With the steady increase in Malomba's importance as a holy city, however, the outward creep of development had brought the place to the hotel's front door and in doing so had swallowed up its grounds. Where the Bank of the Divine Lotus now stood, a centuries-old flamboyant had spread its shade and dripped its flames until a few years ago. The bank had paid fairly if not generously for the site. As Mr Muffy complained at the time with lowered voice, everyone knew the BDL's tentacles spread over the whole country, sucking in revenue from impoverished peasants forced by drought and Chinese price-rigging to take out loans for such things as seed grain and fertiliser. At the least hint of opposition or resistance, though, the same tentacles would strangle the life out of you. Those damned Buddhistic Indians were worse even than the Islamic or Hindu varieties . . .

13

Jason was standing at the door of the bathroom watching the surges and dwindles of grey water coming through the ceiling, hands on narrow hips in a gesture less truculent than resigned. 'What's upstairs?' he asked.

Laki glanced at him with something like sympathy. Most of the travellers he showed into No. 41 had reasons for not being able to protest.

'Nothing. The roof. Where I live.'

'You've got a leak.'

'The women. They are washing in the morning only. Soon finish now. Look,' and to distract his young guest from further contemplation of the room's defects, which included the hot waft of cockroach from the darkness between the floorboards, he indicated the view. Generally speaking, Malomba's architecture was two-storeyed; that and the eminence on which the Nirvana stood meant that little obstructed the prospect of the hills on the far side of town and practically any obtrusion was one of the thirty-nine religious edifices. Prominent in the middle distance was the famous Glass Minaret of the Ibn Ballur mosque. Sunlight winked off its seven hundred and seventy-seven thousand rhomboidal facets. Not far away, at the entrance to the Chinese quarter, rose a cream archway crowned with green upcurving ceramic shingles on whose ridge curveted a pair of golden lions. They sparkled like a dream of fortune. 'You like?'

'It's all right. Why do you live on the roof?'

'Very beautiful. Very fine view. Fresh air. Nobody come except the women to washing for one hour every day. So no disturb.' Pleased to be asked about his domain, Laki said generously, 'I show if you like. We shoot deers together.'

'Deers?'

From a pocket in his cotton uniform the bell-boy fetched out a catapult. Its handle was carved shallowly with a design of tiny flowers and birds, the result of many hours' whittling. From its arms dangled heavy straps of black rubber; its

14

pouch was of oiled leather. It gave off an air of potency which the delicate decoration only enhanced.

'Not bad,' said Jason approvingly. He took it and half-tensed the rubber in an experimental fashion. 'Can you hit anything?'

'Of course. I am expert. The deers in the garden are easy. Not kill but make to jumping. Also one day I to hit Father McGoohan. He walking round and round and read little book so I shoot, *ponk!*, with areca nut. Ha! he is to jumping but not know it me.' Sudden concern crossed Laki's face. 'You not tell Mr Muffy, please?'

'Why should I?' Interest was displacing Jason's fatigue. At that moment a bell pealed faintly in the recesses of the hotel.

'That Mr Muffy. I go now. One day I bring you there and you to trying if also can hit the Fathers.' Laki pocketed the catapult and left. Jason could hear the soft flopping of his rubber sandals echoing down successive flights of the dusty stairs.

✤

Every night at eight o'clock Laki, coming off duty, ate in the kitchen with Raju, who was going on. More accurately, they ate sitting on the threshold of the back door, facing the last greens and madders of sunset. In the sooty cavern at their backs was the bustle of cooking and dishing up. Laki always looked forward to the evening meal, and not merely because he could stuff himself with as much rice and lamb-and-cardamom sausage as he could hold. He liked the gentle philosophical tenor of their conversations, the satisfaction of his own enquiries being met by Raju's considered opinion. Raju clearly enjoyed them, too, for much the same reason.

Finding Raju here at the Hotel Nirvana had been a stroke

15

of fortune indeed. Laki had taken it as a good omen the day he started his apprenticeship. For although they had not known each other, Raju at once recognised the boy's accent and they soon discovered they were from neighbouring villages on the eastern coast and had acquaintances in common. Without a doubt they were distantly related and, as the custom is, where a blood relationship is plausible it is taken as definite. The eighty miles of unspeakable road which separated them from their home province represented exile, further strengthening the bond. What made alliance absolute was their awareness of being self-reliant country-folk at the mercy of scheming townees skilled at nothing but racketeering.

'It's us against that lot out there, my boy,' Raju had told him early on, shying a woody stump of cassava at the kitchen goat and picking fibres from his teeth.

'I know it, uncle.'

'Listen to them. Did you ever hear such a racket?' For as the sun set, most of the thirty-nine assorted temples were passing on the news of this event.

'It's not like this in Saramu, uncle.'

They had both fallen silent, each in his mind's eye seeing the dark coast he had left, with the line of palms along the beach and the huts among them whose oil-lamps and candles outlined in soft orange the rectangles of door and window frames. In the phosphorescent surf boats would be putting out, a pressure lamp lashed to the prow, outriggers smacking and boys wet to the waist dragging themselves aboard like porpoises. Laki could see each familiar detail of his father's face craning over the side of the boat above the reef, the coral heads and outcrops a shadowy green as the light passed above, his elder brother ready with spear or knife while little Gunath paddled gently to keep the bows into the swell. At such moments home-sickness would wring him through and through until his whole being was possessed by the craving to see his mother and sisters again, to go fishing once more with the men. That was what he wanted; that was what he was good at. Wherefore this banishment to a city maddened by traffic and conflicting creeds, whose people couldn't even speak properly?

'I know, boy,' Raju had said as Laki turned his head aside on the doorpost to hide his tears. 'But you'll be going home. We'll save up the bus fare, you and I, then we'll go back with all our hard-earned wealth. And then what parties, what carryings-on! This November, you'll see.'

'It's only March now, uncle.'

'Time passes quickly if you're making money.'

And impossible as it had seemed, the time *had* passed, they *had* gone back to Saramu Province. There had been embraces and parties and cries of admiration at his new shoes, the presents he had brought, the lighter he had given his father which worked without a flint. They all said how he'd grown, how handsome he was becoming. 'Still looks like a goat's hole to me,' his elder brother remarked. 'And I bet this little city gent has forgotten how to fish. He'll be too proud now to go out with the likes of us bumpkins,' which was all that was needed to prove him wrong in the best night's fishing Laki had ever had.

That was more than two years ago. He had been home twice since then, yet for some reason the last time had not been quite so enjoyable. He had done all the old skilful things: had shinned up palms to bring down the toddy morning and evening; had gone fishing; had set off with friends for a day's catapulting and arrived back with a string of small birds at his waist to prove that his competence had not yet rusted away. Hand and eye were still attuned, but behind it all was alteration. He didn't feel much different in himself but could detect a change in others' attitudes. It was less noticeable in the adults, quite marked in the children, in his contemporaries, his old friends. He felt ... not excluded, exactly – certainly not that; but as if a lot had happened in his absence to which he was no longer privy.

17

He was left with the sad conviction that he could never quite catch up now, no matter how much he listened to stories of events. Life at home, he discovered, was maybe not so much a question of knowing who was marrying whom, whose boat had been repossessed by the rural bank for defaulting on a loan, who had been caught giving short measure. It was more a matter of habitual mornings with catapults, nightly fishing, daily choppings of firewood: the constant renewing of bonds, the shared uneventfulness. Once an activity as ordinary as hunting became an occasion, something went out of it which was never to be recaptured save by returning home for good.

He was saddened to perceive that he was looked on as different, as if he were subtly changing his species. To them, evidently, the big bad holy city had him in thrall. Sometimes he let slip words they couldn't understand: perfectly ordinary everyday words for traffic lights or fuse-boxes or similar urban furniture, as well as expressions and oaths which to their ears sounded acrid and vicious instead of meaty. He was asked questions which suggested he might be an alien rather than a brother returned. Little Gunath had said, 'I suppose you'll be considering marriage soon?'; whereas a year ago he would have essayed something a good deal cheekier, a traditional taunt such as: 'Isn't it about time your voice was breaking? I'd be getting worried if I were you,' followed by a squealing chase among the palm trees with additional ribaldries thrown over one shoulder: 'Better try some vine potion' or 'Go and sleep with the Dwarf Princess. They say she brings young boys on.'

But worst of all for Laki was that his very success as a remitter drove an uneasy wedge into affections and friend-ships. He had been sent away to earn money. Very well, then, he was earning money. He earned more as a bell-boy at the Nirvana than his father did from fishing, itself a source of feelings too complex to be spoken about. Yet although he was being the model dutiful son, sending money home to his needy family and thereby deserving the highest approbation, he could not but wonder now and again whether they didn't think more of the money than they did about him. No; that was impossible; of course they wouldn't. But all the same . . .

Finally, he was going to have to do something about the Nirvana. It all boiled down to that. It had been a good job for a boy of eleven or twelve – outstandingly good, even, considering it was his first. But at fourteen or fifteen Laki could see that Mr Muffy was never going to pay him much more than at present. And there was no hope of promotion since there was nothing he could be promoted to. All of a sudden he determined that the upheaval he had undergone should at least be made to pay well. However fondly he had been cut off at the roots, he wanted real compensation. Accordingly he began considering how to set about bettering his lot.

Now, tonight, he said softly to Raju with his mouth full, 'I'm going to leave.'

'Ah. Found something better, then?'

'Not exactly, uncle.'

'Well, boy, do you want the advice of an old man?'

'Of course, uncle. That's exactly what I want.'

'Don't get out of the boat until you've reached land. Easy enough to hand in your notice, but damn silly to do it before you've got somewhere else to go. You can't live on air and if you think Muffy'll give you a month's pay just so's you can bugger off with a pocketful of cash, you've another think coming.'

'Of course not, uncle,' said Laki hastily. It was the very fantasy he'd had.

'Where would you live? You're used to your own room and it costs you nothing. As does this food,' and Raju speared a saffron ball of semolina and popped it into his mouth to make the point. 'You've eaten well here, boy. Grown, too. Skinny little waif you used to be and now look at

19

you, practically a man. Any day now. Well, well; it all goes on. New shoots become old sticks.'

At other times it had been soothing to listen to the familiar proverbs in Raju's mouth but now Laki felt a respectful impatience, a mood further pricked by the old man having confirmed what he had secretly known all along, which was that it would be a mistake to leave his present job for sheer restlessness.

'It needs thinking through,' Raju continued as he chewed. 'You've got a lot in your favour. You know this town well, how it works, and it seems to me you've picked up a good deal of English on the quiet.' He shot the boy a shrewd sidelong look. 'And that was smart. You speak better than I do.'

'Oh no, uncle,' Laki began in confusion.

'You do and you know it. I often wish you were with me on the desk at night when these foreigners turn up. Sometimes I swear I don't understand a word they say. But I'm too old to start learning languages now. I muddle by and that's enough. You're still quick and *willing*. Ah yes, it's having the will which is everything in this life. Once you've lost that you've lost all. But let's proceed. You want to make your fortune, yes? By tomorrow afternoon at the latest?'

'Next week would be soon enough, uncle.'

But unaccountably Raju elected to take this as not quite a joke. 'Maybe you lack ambition after all. I've often thought there's a streak in you of something which might betray you if it gets the better of you.'

'What, uncle?'

'I can't find the word for it,' admitted the old man. 'Luxury, perhaps? Pleasure? *Next week*. A softness, maybe? You'll have to watch that, boy. At any rate I'm convinced if you're to make your fortune you can do it right here in Malomba. You've thought about going somewhere larger – to the capital, for example. Of course; everybody does. But why? You'd simply have to start all over again at the bottom in a strange city, knowing no one and without so much as a stairwell in which to spread your mat. You'd be with the rest of the riff-raff who drift in from all over the country to seek their fortunes. No, much better build on the foundations you've laid here.'

The night porter paused for a draught of palm toddy from the pitcher at his side. The liquor was expensive here in town, and seldom good since it had to be brought in from the coconut plantations in the hills. Toddy did not travel well. A few hours' delay in the hot sun followed by a good sloshing around in a waggon and it turned vinegary and sulphurous. This stuff was fresh and sweet, however, and represented a complicity between them since they tapped it illegally in the Fathers' garden next door. The Fathers themselves seldom ventured beyond the lawn behind their bungalow and hardly ever into the furthest recesses of their estate. But there, virtually hidden among other trees, a group of palms rose so high that their tops were all but invisible from the ground, screened by lower growth. It was Laki who had first had the idea of putting these trees to good use, and now they took it in turns to slip through the fence and collect it. Raju, who still climbed a palm with touching senescent agility, fetched it in the early morning as he came off duty; Laki at night. Had either been caught it would have been all up with them. The police could be relied on to hand out a good beating even before they threw the book at you for evading the state toddy monopoly. After that they would have to settle with the Fathers, and both Laki and Raju had lived in Malomba long enough to know that the last place to expect charity and forgiveness was in a city of divines. Priests and gurus, imams and rabbis, fakirs, mullahs, bishops, brahmins, healers, satanists and all the rest of them: a shifty, gluttonous bunch. That, at least, was their opinion. But then they were animists.

Raju was at this moment drinking deeply of the soul of the palm.

'That's good stuff,' he said and belched softly. 'Just like home. Don't you see, boy? It really makes sense for you to stay in this town because you already know it so well. But there's a better reason still. Money. People go where the money is, that's natural. So they head for the cities. Well, there's money enough in Malomba; there's no need to take a step outside. What's more, it's getting richer. I remember when I first arrived ten years ago this was just another provincial capital – a town which was perfectly ordinary in every way except for having a glut of priests and temples. Nowadays it's got them fit to fart. They say it's always been a great religious centre, but once they started calling it a holy city and drumming up the tourist trade it suddenly became a lot holier. We never used to have all these faith healers and psychic surgeons and what-not. The tourists have brought them in.'

'And they're not doing badly, uncle, are they?'

'They're pissing gold, boy. I'm not saying it works or it doesn't work. I can't say they're all rascals because I don't know. You can't judge a cow by its moo. But I am saying it's a nice little industry they've got going for themselves.'

'Ought I to become a healer then, uncle?'

'No,' admitted Raju, 'I wasn't going that far. Although I suppose we could claim that you're a poor ignorant village boy whose miraculous powers were discovered when he was eight, say. But in practice it wouldn't be as simple as that. First we'd have to find you an agent or protector. I'd guess that the healer market is about saturated at the moment. Tourism's already levelled off and if this guerrilla problem gets any worse it'll drop still further. So that means you'd be competing with all the other healers in town and you know what they're like. They'd smash your elbows with mallets. No, what I was thinking of is more of a way of getting you to make the most of the advantages you have without needing to fake others. Here you are with good health, good English and a good knowledge of town. Now who in Malomba –

22

apart from the Indians and the Chinese, of course – have the real money? Why, the tourists themselves.'

'Ah,' said Laki, comprehending at last. 'You mean I should become a guide?'

'That's a possibility too. Oh, I know what you're thinking, boy – it's only old Raju gassing on, but when's he going to tell me what to do? I shan't, though. I want to give you a kick, that's all.'

'A kick, uncle?'

'Certainly. I know how when a man works he gets into a rut. Day after day he does the same old thing. We go on duty and we go off duty, we go to bed and we eat our meals. But all the time, like as not, the way to something better is staring us in the face. Why does the grouper stay in his hole and grow fat? He doesn't waste his energy swimming about looking for food. He simply waits for food to come blundering in and then he grabs it. He seizes the opportunity, doesn't he?

'The same with you. Look at the guests who come to this hotel. Never mind that if they're richer they may go to the Golden Fortune or the Seven Blessings. Even the poorest hippy is still rich. He's rich enough to travel. He's rich enough to pay for healing sessions or a meditation course or fork out those scandalous ashram fees. We say nothing about his drugs bill, either. What's more, he'll certainly have relatives back home who can lay their hands on real money if things go wrong. You don't need to rip them off, either; you just need to get their confidence. *Never steal a watch when you can steal a heart.* Well, then.'

'It's difficult knowing how to start these things, uncle.'

'Nonsense. Muffy tells me we've got some new guests. Who are they?'

'Some woman and her kids. They're English. Or maybe Italian – but they speak English. She's come for psychic surgery. She says she's got an introduction to *hadlam* Tapranne.'

Raju looked at him triumphantly. 'There you are. She's rich. Remember that Indian film star? Of course she is. Think of those air tickets. She can even afford to bring her children. Big children? Little children?'

'A boy of twelve and a girl of fifteen. She's not bad, the girl. Old Muffy was giving her the eye.'

'Think of going abroad,' said Raju dreamily. 'Imagine getting a job in – for instance – Europe. Or even America,' he added, this being the golden dream to end all others. How they did shimmer, those mythic lands at the ends of impossibly difficult roads which were essentially a never-ending series of toll gates. Roads beset with bribes, extortion, bent recruitment agencies, visa fixers, corrupt passport officials, travel sharks, queues; doors shut at every turn which would open only for hard cash. 'Do you know what I'd do if I were young again?'

'What, uncle?'

'I'd marry a foreigner,' said Raju wickedly.

High in the Apuan Alps between Lucca and Carrara lay the remote village of Valcognano. In common with thousands of other remote Italian villages, it had been abandoned some time after the Second World War. The young men left to look for work, the girls to look for husbands, and the last of the ancients tottered down the mule path to lie in a cemetery near enough to civilisation for little lights to burn beside their names through the harsh winter nights. For twenty years Valcognano was left open to foxes, wild boar and the weather.

Then one day had come a wise man from the East, Swami Bopi Gul, riding in a Boeing, a rented Maserati and finally on a donkey to set up his Community of Pure Light.

Dismounting stiffly, he performed certain rites and meditations and declared the place ideal. It would be a haven of serenity and bliss. Far removed from the impurities and distractions of modern life, the Community's members would drink pure mountain water and warm themselves before fires of chestnut wood from the forests, while relying for illumination on wisdom and kerosene. The kerosene arrived on mule back, together with sacks of flour, jars of oil and other provisions. The wisdom would simply grow of its own accord, declared the Swami, being the bountiful harvest of *Presentness*.

Among the earliest Pure Lighters were the Hemony family; in those days Tessa's husband Bruce had still been around. After the first year or so Swami Bopi Gul's absences became regrettably more protracted as he busied himself with the running of his spiritual empire in places such as Srinagar and Zurich. Consequently the Hemonys and another couple found themselves the elders at Valcognano and newcomers inferred that they had been entrusted by the Swami to carry on the Community's work – as indeed they had.

It is not often appreciated by those who have never lived the simple life up a mountain how complicated it is, nor how much of each day is taken up by tasks of a more or less drudging nature. Many were the young refugees from art and language courses in Florence or Pisa who found their way there hoping to *bliss out* on long hours of sunshine and wine and meditation; but few there were prepared to spend a morning hoeing a maize field or coaxing a refractory mule up the eight hundred and ninety-four broad steps through the chill gloom of the forest. They left, mostly within days, to be replaced by others.

Yet gradually over the years the Community did build itself up until almost all Valcognano's houses had been restored and were lived in by people whose lives – apart from mantras and tantras and curious practices at dawn –

differed very little from those of its original inhabitants. They sowed, they reaped, and often at night they sang songs around the fireside. Curiously, the Pure Lighters were largely free of the problems which typically afflict such enterprises and cause dissent and break-up. There were few scandals and jealousies, while the Italian authorities virtually ignored them. From the outset the Swami had made judicious donations to the parish in whose bailiwick Valcognano was, and the *parroco* was firmly on the Community's side. Every so often he would make the three-hour walk up to the village and satisfy himself that there was no odour of brimstone about the place, no evidence of sorcery, no effigies of horned goats. The inhabitants didn't strike him as practitioners of the black arts, appearing sober and healthy even if a little scruffy and given to expressions of happiness. They certainly plied him most generously with home-made bread, sheep's cheese and cold-extracted oil of hyssop for his stones.

It occurred to the priest to enquire as to the children's education, but he was easily satisfied that they were being well taught since nearly all the adults turned out to have university degrees. Besides, the complications of enrolling them in the state educational system scarcely bore thinking about. The *comune* of which Valcognano was a part would have to send a *scuolabus* to fetch and return them daily, at all seasons and in all weathers. Since it was evident that no *scuolabus* could get up a mule track, the *comune* would have to build a road. Once there was a road there would have to be electricity, telephones, sewage disposal . . . Who knew where such spending would end? And all for an isolated hamlet of self-sufficient folk who treasured their isolation? It was pointless. Far better let the whole matter drop.

So the Italian state left Valcognano to its eccentric but peaceable foreigners, except that every now and then a police helicopter might hover above the maize field to check that nobody had planted marijuana in the middle. As far as officialdom was concerned Jason and Zoe and the other children were as unaccountable as gypsies but of no interest to the law, unlike the genuine gypsy children from Yugoslavia who plagued the peripheral wastelands of Milan and Turin with their pickpocketing rackets.

Theirs had been a strange upbringing, reared as they were in a multicultural limbo. Dal they ate, and polenta and porridge; also curry and pasta, poppadoms, pizza and pudding. They were smallholders with wide horizons, too, for they were always travelling. Tessa would suddenly announce that next week they were going on retreat in Kashmir or to a disciple of the Swami's in Thailand, or merely back to England to dun their capitalist turncoat of a father for more maintenance. Along the way they picked up what they could of formal learning. On the last visit but one Tessa had wangled both children a term's schooling, but Jason especially had proved peculiar and it was not a success.

As for money, well, the Hemonys paid as little attention to it as people do who have never had to worry. Tessa's family were rich; she was an only child. It was true she had married a man without a bean, but he turned out to have a future. They had met at an ashram in Agra where Bruce was wrestling with Sanskrit. He had beads and a glossy clean ponytail, a newly-minted doctorate in biochemistry and a charming smile. Each had recognised the other's spiritual beauty; both were sure the world was best forsaken. Within a year they were married and within two were hurriedly repairing the roof of a tumbledown *casa colonica* in Valcognano – *bliss!* – before autumn turned to winter. But after a few years Bruce had become sad and restless. He was increasingly susceptible to minor ailments which laid him low despite the most skilled aromatherapy and the most elaborate attempts to harmonise his body with Mother Earth. He took to going off on his own for several weeks.

Then one day in spring he returned looking calm and

decisive. He was going to the world (as the phrase had it). He had applied for and got a job as a biochemist working with ICI. Oh yes, and there was one other thing . . . he'd sort of met this girl.

It had been a blow, there was no denying it. For some time Tessa had known Bruce's path had become cloudy, that he was increasingly unable to wipe his spirit clear. But when she told the Swami and he had held her with that wonderful calm gaze of his and smiled his beatific smile, she at once saw it was for the best after all. 'We must each find our own way through the minefield,' was his teaching. 'A seeing person is not always safer than a blind one.' 'But I have a family to support,' said the former public schoolgirl, astonishing herself. 'Support, support? What is support?' asked Gul. He was always a little enigmatic about money matters. He lit a stick of incense and they drank camomile tea sitting together in the bare upper room of a house which had belonged to Valcognano's last midwife. Its walls were now draped with Tibetan prayer flags and Mediterranean sunlight came bounding exuberantly in, bringing with it both excitement and calm. 'Maybe your own path is changing,' he said. 'Who knows?'

'It knows itself,' she said.

What it had known it communicated one night by waking her with the realisation that a job at ICI would bring in a decent sum in maintenance from Bruce, and therefore she needn't rely on the tainted capital of her father's legacy. In a sense she would have earned her alimony; it had all been *meant*, after all. More bliss, except that Zoe had been quite upset by his defection. She had taken valerian for her grief and they had all gone to Sri Lanka for a bit. It had been marvellously restorative, although the poor child had been weepy at first. Jason, perhaps because he was so young, had seemed to accept the whole thing with equanimity. Still, that was all several years ago. Since then Zoe had quite recovered and was rapidly turning into a young woman. Had turned, very probably, at the time when she somewhat lost her head with a naughty boy from LA.

'Well,' thought Tessa with melancholy pride as she leaned on the rotted window-sill of her room in the Hotel Nirvana. She watched the monkeys leaving the sanctuary of the Redemptorist Fathers' garden for their evening pillage of Malomba's outskirts. 'Well, the Hemonys always did have warm hearts. Warm hearts make hot blood, and hot blood makes us *open*. Open to the spirit and new experiences; open to things happening. And that is true freedom – not striving, not grasping. Oh how lucky we are.' She sang a few notes in a little girl's voice, while up from the garden drifted the clotted scent of musk-lilies, the sound of bird-song and snarling monkeys. She had almost forgotten the bleak flash at dawn when for a moment in the bus she had wished above all for her life to be still, her back to be cured, for an end to this road.

But then if someone had ever suggested – trying to account for the occasional sadness which might overtake her as a little cloud crossing her inner sun – that she was a woman of forty with two children and no husband who wandered at whim from one place to the next when not living in a commune up an Italian mountain, she would have replied tartly that if it did not quite comply with bourgeois notions of the purposeful life, then all the more reason to rejoice in it. What precisely *was* so fulfilling about good-consumerism? What so purposeful in being led by the nose for threescore years and ten as a servile member of the admass? Or so self-expressing about stifling beneath that dead weight of conventional impiety?

If as a mother she felt open to accusations that, whereas her own life was her own business, her wayward and untutored children might have little future, she could defend herself with equal vigour. For one thing, Zoe and Jason were anything but uneducated. How many of their contemporaries knew how to make sheep's cheese? Or

29

could recite The Triple Refuge or the Heart Sutra? Or knew to heal a severe burn with lavender oil? In any case they would soon be old enough to go their own ways and if, like Bruce, they wanted to go to the world, there was nothing to stop them. They were not stupid and would soon pick up anything they needed to learn.

Sometimes Tessa could not prevent such rhetorical exchanges from popping into her mind. Although she had long learned to deal with them and was sure she was not wrong, they did trail a fleeting disquiet. She had never liked arguments; they reminded her of fallings-out with her father. It was perfectly reasonable, then, that such things in bubbling up and evaporating should leave behind their residues. And that was not in itself bad. Such sadnesses as one did feel – and only the greatest guru or half-wit would maintain that spiritual exercise rendered one immune to shadows – were proper and could be *used*. They had energies of their own.

Thus she thought, leaning at the window and suddenly prey to the melancholy which comes of arriving exhausted in a strange tropical town early in the morning and lacking the energy to do more than doze fitfully throughout the day. For all her years of travel, and knowing that it was fatal even to think of going to bed, she had once again found herself at eleven in the morning and at three in the afternoon heavy on damp sheets, watching the strips of light between the shutters blaze with white glare and hearing from a remote outer place the cries of children, the creak of carts, the din of people living their lives. She hovered in her darkened room, disengaged, as it might have been without further purchase on her own life and lacking lien on any other.

At this moment her attention was distracted to the little pagoda in the garden beneath. There seemed to be two children playing just inside its darkened doorway. Well, not playing exactly, so much as . . . She leaned further out, a chunk of rot breaking from the sill and floating away trailing

30

dust like cinnamon powder. In this twilight it was hard to see but there really did appear to be two children copulating inside the Fathers' pavilion. And why not too? she thought with a small pang. Bliss. She suspected these people had very clear minds. With such an uncomplicated attitude towards pleasure, there would be no reason to grow up muddied with taboo. That boy Lucky, for example, who had befriended them this morning. He gave off an unmistakable aura of *cleanliness*, of healthy young human animal. Just then a trumpet sounded from up in the sky somewhere to her left, setting off all kinds of bells and gongs and cries. The sudden noise must have startled the children or else it coincided with the end of their lovemaking, for they came hopping out of the pagoda's window and loped across the lawn with their tails in the air.

It was her laughter which chased away the last of Tessa's doldrums and, since she was supporting herself on shaking arms, provoked the final collapse of the entire window-ledge which broke off in a cloud of termite-casts and fell like balsa wood. This made her laugh even more. Malomba was to be playful after all. Suddenly the vibrations were good. It was going to be numinous and playful. After a shower, during which she sang in her cement stall beneath a weak stream of rusty water, she felt ready for anything.

Morning. Laki was returning from an unsuccessful raid on the bus station. Another overnight bus from the capital had arrived, but although there were several foreigners aboard none had guest-potential so far as the Nirvana was concerned. There was a group of Buddhist monks from Burma wearing orange robes and carrying yellow umbrellas who stood equably around on the packed-down vegetable waste. Suddenly a black Mercedes had nosed its way through the crowds, driven by a monk wearing smoked glasses and tailored robes. Inside the rear window two stickers in elegant script were legible through the tinted screen. One read 'Support Your Local Temple' and the other 'Remember The Five Precepts'. The monks climbed in with smiles and were whisked away. This left a large and sinister-looking negro with a pockmarked face whose hands shook. Laki overheard him asking for 'Vudusumin'; and since *sumin* was the word for 'temple', and the commonest suffix of any destination in Malomba, he drew his own conclusions.

Nothing daunted he dawdled in the general direction of the hotel, sniffing the breeze. In a town where a section of the populace forever wore expressions of pious dignity he stood out like a tiger in a garden. His hair shone in the early sun, he walked with a spring, his eyes gleamed. Shop-keepers busy rolling down the mouths of sacks the better to display their different qualities of rice and chick-peas and mulva meal would glance up as he passed, alerted as if by the flashing of a mirror.

'Morning there, Laki-boy. No catch today?'

'Not yet, Mr Hussein. I don't know where the tourists have all gone.'

'Thailand, I heard. Or was it India?'

'It's the Troubles.'

'Stupid things. They're perfectly safe in Malomba if they only knew it. The worst that ever happens to tourists here is getting fleeced by holy men.'

'Or being cursed, Mr Hussein.'

On all sides the commercials of Malomba were opening their shutters. The scent of freshly baked *laran* bread drifted along the street like a wraith over the dust and dung and amber puddles of donkey stale. Laki stopped and bought four of the feathery, conical loaves dusted with crushed sesame. In the bakery's dark interior he glimpsed another boy in a white apron and waved, but the boy was too busy raking embers out of the clay oven to notice.

He reached the gateway to Chinatown, whose pillars bore an inscription proclaiming that it was a symbol of the eternal friendship, esteem and co-operation between Malomba City Council and the Chinese Chamber of Commerce. Overhead the golden lions pranced and snarled at the swallows. Laki remained puzzled by their teeth. Whoever saw a lion with teeth like dowels? How could you rend flesh with a mouthful of pegs? In the blue sky beneath each upraised paw, between the curling red tongues, through the arch of each belly, birds flickered and darted. Beyond the gateway itself was a vista of *dim sum* restaurants and dry goods merchants, the signs with their vertical strings of characters receding in a jumble of red and gold. But Laki's attention was fixed elsewhere, on a strange building standing apart in its own grounds just outside the Chinese quarter.

This was a temple, he knew, one of the handful in which tourists or any other visitors were not welcome. It was in the form of a squat, whitewashed ziggurat peaking in a suggestive little tower capped in vermilion. The whole building was quite small and had about it the air of being designed to prevent anything from leaking out. The successive blocks of diminishing size reminded him of the piles of weights on top of the pressure-cookers on sale in Chinatown. This temple stood back from the road behind heavy iron gates he had seldom seen open. There was a low wall surmounted by more iron fencing high enough to lose itself in the lower leaves of several lettuce trees whose drizzling gums and resins turned the pavement beneath them black and tacky before the monsoon. The grounds visible within were heavily overgrown, dark with foliage and tangled with vines. Among it all, gourds and blooms burned like sultry flames. There was no notice on the gate, no inscription over the blockhouse's narrow doorway, nothing to tell the curious passer-by that this was indeed a house of worship rather than a ponderous tomb.

Thanks to his friendship with Mr Tominy Bundash, an official guide who carried a plastic ID card in a leather wallet to prove it, Laki knew something of this mysterious place although he quite badly wanted to know more. One memorable afternoon eighteen months ago in the Nirvana's kitchen, he had questioned the guide and learned it was known as the Lingasumin, its full title being 'First Tantric Temple of the Left-Handed Shaktas, Malomban Rite'.

'As you are doubtless aware,' Mr Tominy Bundash had said in his official voice, 'Tantrism or Tantric Buddhism originated in mediaeval India. Its adherents strive to attain liberation through two principal means: firstly by the repetition of sacred phrases culled from the Tantric scriptures known as *dharani*, and secondly by the yogic practice of sexual intercourse. The Malomban Rite here, due to migratory patterns over the last century, is more Hindu than Buddhist and characterised by "left-handed-ness" or the antinomian doctrine that a human being is beyond such petty matters as good and evil and –'

'Sexual intercourse?' Laki interrupted incredulously. 'Did you say sexual intercourse?'

'I did, boy. They believe that the height of religious experience is the utter bliss of ritual sexuality.'

'You mean it's a *religion*? Can anyone join?'

'I have no idea,' said the guide loftily. 'However, I'm assured by my good friend the Mayor's brother, Mr Botiphar, that they're a sect of considerable austerity and self-control. For example, they completely abjure drinking and smoking. But I digress. One of the classic Tantric practices involves union with a *shakti* or spiritual wife, but in the Malomban Rite it is considered an act of greater devotion to the deity to have union promiscuously with social inferiors – one cites for scriptural precedent the love of Lord Krishna for the milkmaid, Radha – or with others of the same sex. Practices include the so-called black ritual in which a corpse is induced to ejaculate, rarefied techniques of self-stimulation and ways of greatly enlarging the male member of regeneration.'

'What's that?'

His informant descended with some exasperation. 'That's your cock, you stupid boy.'

'No, I mean, what's the technique?' Although it was a fact that the very conversation was proving efficacious with Laki.

'I can't possibly say,' said Mr Bundash. It was not clear as to whether he spoke out of discretion or ignorance. 'I am emphatically not a member of this sect; I am a good Moslem. It is merely part of my profession to know facts about the buildings and customs of Malomba which would be of interest to a visitor. I'm hardly an expert on the finer points of very alien religious doctrines. But since you ask, I believe it involves caterpillar hair.'

Thereafter whenever Laki passed the building he felt a certain quickening of the blood. Indeed, on mornings like this full of sunlight and irradiating energy, he felt positively drawn to it so that later it would seem his steps had turned of their own accord to make the detour which enabled him to loiter past on the sticky pavement, eyes trying to pierce the heavy stonework and glimpse esoteric rituals inside. Say what you like about Malomba, he agreed with himself as he finally headed for home with his loaves, it was full of interest and strange things.

'How slow I am this morning,' Mr Muffy greeted him from behind the desk where he was reading his stars. 'I had some silly idea you'd gone off looking for guests, but all along it was bread you were after.'

'No tourists, Mr Muffy. Good morning, Mr Muffy. No tourists at all. So I bought something to make our own guests happy so they will stay here longer and bring in more money.'

Behind him he heard the proprietor's newspaper rattle

sourly as he turned into the dining room. He had surmised correctly: the Hemonys were at table, tackling large slices of papaya.

'Good morning, my lady, miss,' he inclined his head cheerfully. 'Good sleeping, I hope?'

'Oh, Lucky, good morning to you. Yes, thank you; we all had a wonderful sleep. I'm afraid we slept most of yesterday too.'

But Laki had spotted something amiss.

'What is this?' he cried, dumping his bread on an adjacent table and picking up their toast with horror. 'This no good. Very old. No, no, is not for eating. Look, I take,' and he removed the entire supply in handfuls, replacing it with his fresh loaves. 'I buy this now,' he explained. 'Very new. Still hot, you feel. Special Malomba bread, we call *laran*. I buy to you, my lady, because you guest.'

'How lovely. What did you say it was called? *Laran?*'

This dining room gave on to a small verandah. Not so many years ago it had overlooked a lawn dotted with magnolia trees, but nowadays it mostly backed on to the BDL's yard. Still, being open to the air it was moderately cool and tumbling finches flew in and out, pecking up crumbs and clinging upside down to the fly-spotted blades of the motionless ceiling fan. One of these birds was now perched on top of a cracked mirror advertising a soft drink and was fervently attacking its own image. Laki left the room with a deferential smile as the Hemonys started their loaves, flakes of crust splitting like shrapnel on to the floor to the interest of the finches whose shrill cries brought still others swooping in.

Leaving behind him the sound of an aviary, he went to the kitchen where he prepared a small brazier shaped like a round-bottomed saucepan with holes in it. Then, starting at the top of the building, he fumigated the occupied rooms one by one, shaking powdered incense on to the coals from a beer tin. Wreathed in fragrant smoke he paid special attention to No. 41 where the smell of mould was strongest. On the floor beneath he knocked on Zoe's door before letting himself in. He walked all round the room with the brazier at arm's length describing a thick smoke-ring, while his eyes took in the rumpled bed, the T-shirt and underwear hung up to dry. Through the open window came the comfortable sound of broody hens clucking on the bank's roof.

With a last stare at the underwear Laki sighed and gave the brazier a valedictory waft, shutting the door softly behind him. She certainly was beautiful. Seeing them all together at breakfast just now had given him quite a lurch. Maybe it was just the morning sunlight, but it seemed to him their blond heads had lit up the room, so bright was their hair. The lady's of course, was not quite so fine and lustrous, having – as he noticed when standing over her with the loaves – somewhat browner roots, as well as strands of grey which veiled it in a certain mistiness. The boy's was, if anything, fairest of all. Laki was much intrigued by fair hair. Since his own was the uniform jet-black of all his country-men, anything different had about it a touch of exoticism, while blondness like the Hemonys' carried with it the golden air of purest Hollywood fantasyland. Maybe Zoe was after all a princess travelling incognita. Perhaps – an awful thought – perhaps it was *she* who had to visit *hadlam* Tapranne for psychic surgery? Maybe the publicity which would otherwise surround her made it necessary to travel disguised as an ordinary person?

But here they were, coming up from breakfast and catching him with the brazier in one hand and the pass-key in the lock of Mrs Hemony's door. So convinced had he become by his own tale that Laki noticed with surprise how extraordinarily well Zoe looked and thought how bravely she dissembled.

'Excuse please, my lady. I am for incensing your room.'

'What a lovely smell. It's all over the hotel.'

'At least it couldn't make my room smell any worse,' said Jason.

'Jay! Don't be so ungrateful to our friend. You ought to say thank you to Lucky.'

Laki opened the door for them and followed them in with his brazier. He blew on the coals and sprinkled the pinkish powder. Smoke billowed up. Tessa wafted a little towards her nose with one hand.

'Frankincense,' she said. 'Yes, definitely olibanum. Camphor and sandalwood. A trace of myrrh, perhaps. But there are citrus tones as well, don't you think?' Her children remained silent. 'Neroli? No, I know. It's like that one in Kuala Lumpur, you remember? Where you had the nose-bleed, Jason? The man burned it for you to inhale and it worked at once. That had dried pomelo rind ground up in it. The burnt marmalade smell? This is the same. Oh, and of course, benzoin – or some sort of styrax. All right, Lucky; you tell us what it's got in it.'

'I don't know, my lady. I buy in market only. Quality three because Mr Muffy not like to spending.'

'Honestly, Mum, you take everything so *seriously*,' said Zoe.

'Well, I like to know,' Tessa told her stoutly. 'Such things are important. Every day you do like this, Lucky?'

'Oh yes, my lady. Every morning. Bring good fortune, make all bad spirits go away.'

'Very proper too. Make sure you do it thoroughly around my bed, please.' Laki pulled the bed away from the wall and sandwiched himself behind the wormeaten headboard, dutifully asperging smoke. 'Oh – and Lucky? You mustn't keep calling me "my lady". My name is Tessa. I'm not a peeress; just plain Mrs Hemony.'

'Yes, missus.'

'And Lucky – I'm afraid I've a little confession to make. Here,' she beckoned him over to the window. 'Last night I broke the sill.'

'No, missus. You not break; it fall by himself. Very old and bad wood. I tell Mr Muffy make new.'

'You tell Mr Muffy I don't mind whether he mends it or not, but that I shall of course pay him for the damage.'

Jason, who had been idly rolling his mother's little brown bottles of essential oil up and down the bed, asked, 'Is there a swimming pool anywhere?'

'Of course there isn't,' said Zoe. 'This is a Third World country. Where do you think we are, Italy?'

'We'll go to the coast just as soon as we've finished here, Jay. Promise. Anyway, it's time we went exploring Malomba. I'm so excited. Yesterday was rather a write-off. Lucky, can we get a map here in the hotel?'

'Mr Muffy have map. Also have names of guides. You be careful, missus. Many evil fellows in Malomba, fake guides have no ID – take you to bad place, then to robbing you. Camera, passport, watch, shoeses. Steal all money then leave. Careful-careful.'

If this warning did not exactly accord with Tessa's preconceptions of life in a holy city, then neither did it come as much of a surprise. She had done a lot of travelling.

'I very good guide,' Laki was suggesting shyly. 'Only I have duty here.'

'Yes, Mum, why don't we borrow Lucky?' asked Zoe, causing him an electric shock of pleasure which made the handle of the still-smouldering brazier tingle. 'At least we know he's honest.'

Laki flashed his glance on her. 'I honest, miss. I am trusting your life. But not always free. When I not free I give you name of very good Moslem man, my friend Mr Tominy Bundash. He official guide to Malomba. Have ID. He show temples, fire-walking, spirit healing, everything.'

As Laki went out Jason looked expectantly up at him from his bottles and caused the bell-boy to think that his, at any rate, was a boredom which might be exploited. Things were looking promising. Had not the missus already called him 'our friend'? And had not the beautiful Zoe asked for him personally – personally! – as their guide?

❧❀❧

For the next day or two the Hemonys explored Malomba without the help of Mr Bundash, perhaps out of loyalty to Laki who meanwhile lost no opportunity to perform his discreet services. In such matters he showed imagination and tact, knowing that to display too much eagerness would work against him. To be obliging was one thing, but he had learned that Europeans in particular became suspicious of too much solicitude. He supposed this was a sad reflection on the state of affairs at home.

Zealously he fumigated their rooms, going to some trouble in arranging to be doing it at the very moment his guests returned. He was seen leaving Tessa's room with a carpenter's rule and hammer. 'To fixing window for missus,' he said gravely, padding away up the corridor with a preoccupied air. Although she looked and found no evidence of repairs, she was touched that he had remembered, especially in a town whose predominating attitude was what she would have described as 'laid back'.

She and the children were doing a lot of walking. They bought a map and did the sights, visiting (it seemed to Jason) a hundred and seventy-three temples for each iced Mango Surprise consumed.

'The map must be wrong,' he said while waiting for one of these rare delicacies to be served. 'Look, they say there are thirty-nine temples in Malomba. We've already been to more than that this morning.'

'How silly you are,' said Zoe.

'And,' persisted Jason, looking closely at the legend, 'it says several of those are shut to visitors. The Vudusumin,

40

for example. The Masonic Lodge – and this Lingasumin thing. I expect they're the only interesting ones.'

'You liked the Glass Minaret,' said Tessa.

'It was all right. It wasn't *made* of glass, though, was it? Just covered with bits of mirror.'

'And the stuffed man.'

'Yes, the stuffed man was okay.'

They had found him in the House of Rimmon, a circular building where all male visitors were required to remove their shirts. The entire floor was knee-deep in straw symbolising – according to the printed explanation – the threshing floor on which all human souls will one day be winnowed. Standing in the middle was a small brown man, stark naked and holding a flail in one upraised hand. Around his brow was a circlet of gold from which arose wavy jags like bent spearheads, alternately copper and gold. These were the tongues of fire with which the unrighteous chaff would be burned.

Until the guide-book told her that the man with the flail was believed to be at least a thousand years old, Zoe had been embarrassed lest he caught her staring. Whatever preservation process he had undergone had resulted in an extraordinarily lifelike skin texture quite different from the dried-parchment look of mummification. He was supposed to be completely stuffed with emmer and barley, and at this very moment university departments in Europe and America were studying minute samples of skin reverently taken from the soles of his feet in order to date him. The Stockholm Institute of Forensic Science had also taken scrapings from under the toenails of one foot, and from their analysis of particles of mud, pollen and camel dung were able to confirm that they were consistent with an Eastern Mediterranean provenance. The Rimmonites of Malomba were already overjoyed and preparing for immense celebrations when the news arrived – as they never doubted it would – proving this figure to be the The God

Himself, immeasurably older than anybody else's, whose last corporeal manifestation happened to be that of a man who had fled Damascus before the spread of Islam.

Tessa had tried, as she tried in every temple she visited, to be responsive to the vibrations, to the particular brand of the numinous which the place diffused. It was not easy with Jason giggling and shirtless, but the light did fall quite beautifully from a clerestory of unglazed slits around the shallow dome. Motes and spicules stirred up from the crackling straw danced in its beams. The whole place had the warm, immemorial smell of hay-lofts. Even though the figure of Rimmon was not perhaps quite as awesomely menacing as intended – having the stature of a modern eleven-year-old – there was something engrossing about his antiquity, his silence, his posture. Indeed, the more she looked at him and saw a man engaged in a timeless human activity, the more he seemed to transcend the role and emit a stealthy power. Altogether Tessa had been quite sorry to leave the House of Rimmon.

The Mango Surprises arrived, macédoines of mango and soursop with a dusting of mauve hundreds-and-thousands. Thus fortified – and in Jason's case appeased – they made their way to the Wednesday Market next to the bus station. The alleys were thronged with people who carried the Hemonys along as if they had plans for them before dumping them at a street corner piled with the spare parts of car engines. Gamely they rejoined the crowd and were borne off again in a different direction, past heaps of trussed chickens with their beaks agape. There were boys with cloth wrapped around their heads seated behind pyramids of green mangoes. For those stopping to refresh themselves, the boys also dispensed salt to sprinkle on the unripe fruit. A few steps further and they came upon live fish sliced lengthwise to the spine and laid out with ice on draining slabs so that the monger could demonstrate the freshness of his wares. Their hearts twitched, their lifeblood streamed, their flotation sacs pumped and inflated hopelessly. Black silk Chinese caps in conference over the fish; long robes, yellow monkish robes. Priestly robes and cotton pantaloons delicately hitched to pass over improvised duckboards and broken packing-cases which might afford unspattered passage across pools of ordure. And suddenly, with the abruptness of silence unaccountably falling, the family were out on the other side. They found themselves beached at the end of a boulevard lined with balsam oaks whose perfume-drenched candles tottered away down the perspective towards the outer suburbs. Immediately before them stood a tall man dressed in purple, holding a slender leather pouch.

'Nasal hygiene?' he enquired in English. When nobody responded he said to Tessa, 'I am picking your nose please, madam.' He withdrew from the case what looked like a pair of slender chopsticks but which on closer inspection proved to be freshly peeled twigs with sharpened points.

'No,' said Tessa. 'Thank you all the same.'

'You mean,' Jason wanted to know, 'you're a *professional* nose-picker?'

'I am, young sir,' said the man with a bow. 'Very noble profession. In your country I am not knowing the custom. Here in Malomba it very bad to putting finger in nose outside house. Maybe go blind. But wooden piece is okay. So we are doing.'

Looking round, Jason noticed another man in purple standing a few yards off. This one had a customer whose chin he held in one hand, tilting the head back to face the sun while with the other he delicately manipulated the twigs. Then he withdrew them and having flicked them towards the kerb wiped them on a strip of cloth. Tessa had already been upset by the fish, and now another fragment of her former private-school self bobbed up.

'Most quaint,' she said. 'Come along.'

Turning, they entered the crowd once more and were

milled about amid hubbub and confusion before being spat from beneath the Chinatown arch. 'Oh, I wish it was next Thursday,' said Zoe. 'Can't we go and see this healer before then?'

'I'm afraid not, Zo. It was difficult enough getting any appointment at all. *Hadlam* Tapranne is probably the most sought-after healer in Asia. Of course, the Teacher engineered it all.' This, to be sure, was Swami Bopi Gul. 'How that divine man surrounds us with light. How lucky we are!'

'But that's at least another week,' Jason objected.

'I know it is, Jay. But we'll find lovely things to do, happy things. You'll see. Look at it,' she threw a hand largely at the sky in a gesture which took in the dazzling blue, the green-tiled arch with its gold lions, the variegated tumult through which they had just passed. It also took in the First Tantric Temple of the Left-Handed Shaktas, Malomban Rite, crouching among its vines over the road.

Zoe heard her catch her breath. 'Is your back bad, Mum?'

'It's perfect,' said Tessa. 'Or nearly. All the same, though, I'd rather like to spend this afternoon in the Botanical Gardens. The book says they're spectacularly beautiful. There's a Buddha and a butterfly house and a meditation grove. That sounds restful after this morning.'

'I don't want to come,' said Jason.

'Well, you've got to,' his sister told him.

They had a conciliatory lunch in a Chinese restaurant.

'Then what would you like to do instead?'

'We could go on the train.' This was a miniature railway which was apparently laid out around the boundary of the Botanical Gardens. 'Then you could go and look at your butterflies and meditate and things.'

'He's so spiritual,' Zoe said.

'The spirit affects us in different ways at different ages,' her mother observed, expertly picking a raisin from a pile of rice with her chopsticks. 'And you'd go back to the hotel?'

'Probably,' said Jason.

Malomba was not a large town and there was little which could not be reached on foot. Twenty minutes' walking and they arrived at the park. Here was a blistering expanse of coarse tropical grass worn to the roots and dotted with trees which gave off a subtly depressed air of not yet having been felled as opposed to having been encouraged to grow. Packed densely in the shade between them Malomban couples were sitting. Across the wastes between these oases plodded ice-cream vendors, their aluminium boxes slung over one shoulder, and children selling newspaper screws of unshelled peanuts. A few hundred yards away a belt of forest trees marked the beginning of the Botanical Gardens, which seemed to merge with the coconuts and bamboos of the closer foothills.

Directly in front of the Hemonys was a miniature railway station, bizarrely stylised to look like an English country halt – Adlestrop, perhaps – complete with raised platforms and white picket fencing. Waiting at it, exhaling gently, stood a little green steam-engine with a dour Malomban in a peaked cap hunched on its tender, a heap of firewood at his back. Coupled to it were three open carriages with tin benches and canvas awnings. Several families were sitting patiently with their children, sucking soft drinks from polystyrene cups whose straws poked through their lids.

'And this is what you wanted to go on?'

'Why not?' said Jason. While Tessa bought the tickets he went to look at the engine and exchange a few words with the driver. 'It's Taiwanese,' he informed them, climbing aboard.

'I hope that makes you feel better.'

'Don't nag, Zo,' her mother said gently.

'But Mum, this is for *children*.'

'No, it's not,' Jason told her. 'It's for people who don't want to see butterflies and meditate.'

A guard's whistle sounded, a tiny signal fell, the engine

driver unslumped and tooted a shrill blast which sped flatly across the park, and they were off. It was, even Zoe had to admit, agreeable and even quite restful in its own way. The engine chuffed, the wheels made a subdued iron clicking, they never went faster than a brisk trot. Now and then as the track wove around the trees small boys would detach themselves from the shade and race alongside, generally outpacing the train for a few yards before dropping behind and returning proudly to their families.

As the breeze fanned a smell of hot oil, steam and smuts back over the passengers, Tessa thought it was almost certainly the first time either of her children had been on a steam train. She remembered her own childhood and how steam engines from Victoria Station had carried her off to school on the south coast of England. She had hated them then, but today this little model was bringing back all sorts of marginal nostalgias which emerged into the foreign sunshine like wisps of smoke from a tunnel's mouth. Then the rueful censor chided. 'No,' she told herself, 'no. That was nearly *thirty years* ago. That happened to someone else entirely. To hanker after the past is just another form of grasping. Let go. It only gets in the way, it can do you no good. It holds us back.'

Among the trees inside the Botanical Gardens she glimpsed a flash of the thirty-foot-high Golden Buddha which had been brought overland from Thailand five centuries earlier by ox-cart and river ferry. She had read that wherever its haulers had rested for the night, a shrine had been built to commemorate its passing. Now it sat at the end of a lotus pool beneath a *ficus religiosa* which had been lovingly grown from a cutting of the very Bo-tree at Bodh Gaya in India under which Gautama had achieved enlightenment and become the Buddha. Her eyes watered a little at the thought. The beauty of the story of the Buddha's enlightenment always had that effect on her, as did reflecting on the depth and subtlety of the Dhamma. It was

46

utterly mysterious, yet not at all mystifying since there need be no deities to mess things up, no sacraments like the ghoulish rituals in which Christians indulged – just the power of the human mind to transcend this earth and find its own way to bliss. As Tessa had said to herself at the time of her conversion in Nepal the year Zoe was born, by their symbols shall ye know them. Who would not ally themselves with a philosophy represented by the still, rapt figure of a contemplative rather than with a religion whose sign was a gibbet? She recalled that at this very moment, back in the glooms of Europe, Easter was only a week away. Here, steeped in heat and scent and light, Malomba was ebulliently un-Lenten.

These reflections were interrupted by a series of piercing whistles from the engine and a shuddering of brakes which sent hands out automatically for support. A screaming yelp sounded nearby and a mongrel dog appeared running at a hobble diagonally away from the train. One of its forelegs ended midway and it was an instant before Tessa took in that the accident was happening *now*, that the screaming dog was trailing behind it a bright scatter of crimson blood across the tawny grass, that even at this moment they were trundling over its severed paw. From up front the driver was looking back at his passengers with a grin, shaking his head at the hopelessness of dogs which lay dozing with their legs on railway lines. By now he had released the brakes and the animal was eighty yards away, stopping momentarily to bite at its stump. It went on again but more lethargically and soon halted once more, head to leg. The puffing of the engine turned hollow; the train was passing into a tunnel made of green-painted tin with a brick portal. The last glimpse Tessa had was of the dog crumbling, melting downwards, a lone lump on the baked width of park.

Jason made his own way back to the hotel, leaving his mother and sister to recover among the diverse balms offered by the Botanical Gardens. The streets were hot and drowsy. At times he was sure he fell asleep as he walked; whenever he tripped over a pothole it was as if he woke up to recover his balance. Some way off the Glass Minaret winked and blazed above the slums and boulevards, a celestial conductor down which a tithe of the abounding light and energy of the solar system might pucker and pass to this dark earth. On it Jason fixed his lethargic eye and navigated in a trance.

The air of Malomba was saturated with odours. Fragrances of fruit rotting in the Wednesday Market mingled with those of a thousand balsam oaks, orchid sapodillas, belfry palms. From the clustered violet bells of these last trees tolled heavy notes of scent, rolling out of merchants' gardens and temple grounds. To Jason, reeling with perfumes, there was one single smell behind all the others which in a few short days had become for him that of Malomba itself. He had no idea what it was.

He entered Chinatown. In stenching alleys behind the restaurants dogs were fighting over the lunchtime crop of puppy bones and fish heads. Gradually he became aware of a voice calling him, together with a hollow grinding noise. Looking down he found himself addressed by the torso of a boy mounted on castors. Of much the same age, this young fellow had a pair of muscular arms and hands wrapped in filthy cloths with which he rowed himself along. To each corner of his wood pallet were nailed steel bearings, worn ball-races discarded by mechanical workshops. In stopping he had slewed himself with a burst of sparks and blocked the path so Jason somehow lacked the energy to walk round him. Then in a high voice the boy-torso began to sing.

Thought flew out of Jason's head, his feet would not stir. He watched the white, glittering teeth, the two grubby lumps of hand held out towards him, was fixed by the eyes which never left his face. The song climbed the hot walls of the alley and floated towards the pigeons slicing the blue air overhead. There was in it none of the shocking nakedness which singing on a street ordinarily had when upraised against the din of traffic, the indifference of passers-by. On the contrary, the boy's voice blotted out all background noise so that he became cocooned in its sweetness.

How hot it was! It seemed there was nothing but this immense heat and the singing, interdependent in some way. *Sima.* The knot of mongrels foraging and brawling at the alley's end were balletic in their movements. *Sima.* Not a sound came from them, only their feet raised whirlpools of dust, their fangs gleamed mutely. *Sima sima sima.*

Jason found the singing had stopped and the boy was addressing him.

'*Sima?*' The wrapped hands were still extended and now he saw they held several small brown lumps.

'I don't speak . . . I don't know . . .' he stumbled and suddenly his feet were free and he could walk away. A last *sima* behind him and then silence in which he heard only his own footsteps. At the mouth of the alley he looked back and the boy-torso had not moved. Then with an abrupt thrust of his knuckles he spun on his trolley with a screech of steel and rowed away at a great pace, dusty thatch of hair flapping, the sound of his wheels fading into the snarling of dogs.

Laki had been alternately dozing and plotting beneath the vine's shade on the very edge of the roof. Fresh bread, fumigations and repairs were a good start, but minor services needed to become favours, obligation turn into intimacy. How did one insinuate oneself into the closed circle of a family's affections? It was precisely this delicate insertion he had been pondering when suddenly he caught sight of the son down below in the street. Thoughtfully he watched the boy enter the hotel alone.

And so it was that a few minutes later when Jason opened

the door of Room 41 he found the bell-boy standing on the bedside table tearing handfuls of beard from the ceiling.

'Make repair,' Laki greeted him succinctly. But Jason threw himself on to his bed with the exhaustion of one embarking on a long illness. 'You okay? Where missus and miss?'

'Botanical Gardens. I'm thirsty.' He reached for an empty glass on the floor at his bedside and going to the tap turned it on. It sighed.

'No water now, five o'clock coming back. But not for drinking. Malomba water very bad.' Laki jumped off the table. 'I get *you* cold drink, anything you want. Coca Cola-Bolly-Pepsi-Mops-Fanta-Seven-Up.'

'Mops?'

'Local drink only. Moslems making. Too much sweet, too many gas.' He went to the window and tossed out the netted tuft of roots and rot he had pulled from the wound in the ceiling. Through Jason's mind came and went a terrifying image of his mother's forthcoming operation. He fixed his eyes on Laki's hands.

'Where's your catapult?' He mimed pulling back elastic.

'Ah, *kancha*.' Laki drew the weapon half out of his pocket. Its pouch lolled. 'Always here,' he said. 'I go now to fetching soft drinks, then I show my house upstairs. We make *kancha*.'

For the ten minutes he was away Jason fell into a deep, imageless sleep. From beyond the window came faint sounds of the world through which he had just passed. It was so full of violent toxins and pungencies, so inescapable in its heat that one might almost have supposed the city had plans for him, for all his family, that a process of softening-up had already begun. Why else should belfry palms toll out their scent, the parakeets swarm in the cloud-tree in the Redemptorist Fathers' garden? For what else the massed fairyland of temples, churches, mosques and synagogues? While somewhere behind it all were the healers, the therapists, the psychic surgeons maybe sharpening their thumbnails, maybe hiding slivers of razor-blade beneath them, maybe just honing their powers. The only certain thing was that they were waiting.

Jason opened his eyes. Laki was softly bouncing the catapult's dangling pouch on his chest. In his other hand the bell-boy held a pair of bottles by their necks. 'Come,' he said and Jason obeyed. He glided without feeling the floor, following Laki to the dark end of the corridor where they went through a door. This gave on to back stairs ascending from spicy gloom. A further flight led upwards, something of an afterthought maybe, since the treads were of hastily-laid soft brown bricks between which bulged unpointed mortar.

They emerged from a hatchway into the blows of the sun. Jason stood stupefied by the encircling panorama, by the radiance of the Glass Minaret, by the thirty-nine temples and four cinemas with canopies of trees boiling up between them as if their veins were stuffed with pure hydrogen. Laki was unlocking the door of a tumbledown mud-brick shed and motioning him inside in a proprietorial way. It was a limewashed cell, surprisingly cool and lit mainly from a hole in the roof through which a dense vine was thrusting. This knotty plant came from low down one wall, filled half the room, went out through the ceiling and curved over again to hang a tangling freight of gourds and leaves over the edge of the hotel roof and form a shady pergola outside.

'It's really a good room,' said Jason admiringly. He accepted a cold bottle and drank. From the dimness beyond the vine came the sound of pigeons; curved flakes of white down drifted through the sunbeams. But more than anything else he noticed the smell, that same smell he had thought characterised the town. But here it was concentrated, almost glandular. Surely this very room was the heart of Malomba? Like a tomato plant the vine bore fruit and flowers at the same time. It was as if it were simultaneously mature and immature. Its gourds were pale and warty, the flowers most brilliant cadmium yellow, each with a central dot of indigo. Jason went to it and held its branches and the scent of the flowers poured over him so that for an instant he was on the point of blissful anaesthesia.

Laki stood watching his visitor with a look of pride. 'Good house?' he asked at length.

'I've never seen a room with a tree in it before.' He was reluctant or unable to let go of the branches.

'National Plant: *karesh*. *Karesh* in English is "vine".'

'It's not like any vine I've ever seen,' said Jason doubtfully, thinking of the vines of Valcognano which rampaged like weeds along the brinks of abandoned terraces and in autumn hung their pounds of grapes over the abyss. Italy was suddenly very far off, rugged and prosaic. Simple though his own room at home was, it had none of the bareness of this cell with its straw mat on the floor in one corner. On the other hand there was an extreme richness here which his own room lacked, an exotic self-containment that amounted to luxury. A few articles were lodged here and there among the leaves: a piece of mirror, a coconut shell of soap ends, a clean shirt, a short knife acutely curved as if for pruning.

'Knife for making toddy,' explained Laki. 'Each time to fetching must to cut again very thin piece.'

'Oh,' said the boy, understanding not at all.

As if he had suddenly remembered it was wiser to be discreet about his tapping activities, even in front of a foreigner who plainly hadn't a clue, Laki sidetracked the conversation abruptly by stabbing a gourd. Instantly a bleb of clear liquid gathered at the wound and descended in a long, swinging drool towards the floor. 'Sticky,' he said, touching the filament and making threads between his fingertips.

'Can you eat them?' Jason asked.

'No, not to eating.' Laki produced his catapult once more. 'We try *kancha* outside now?'

52

As Tessa had discovered, the Nirvana backed on to the lush and largely unfrequented garden of the Redemptorist Fathers. Laki led the way across the roof, pointing out the shallow cement trough by the tap where the women did their washing to the discomfort of Room 41's occupants. The area was crisscrossed with wires from which hung threadbare sheets stamped with the hotel's name. After stopping to pick some pebbles from the mud of the dovecote's walls, Laki squatted by the low parapet and pointed. Far below, one of the Fathers' deer was grazing near the pagoda, a buck whose antlers shone in the sun. He fitted a stone into the pouch, drew a bead, and let fly. The deer leaped and bolted. There came the distant rattle of stone off antler.

'Golly,' breathed Jason, the hum of the pebble through the air still in his ears.

There followed some ten minutes of tuition, at the end of which he could hit the pagoda with pieces of gravel four times out of ten.

'One year to practising,' Laki told him with pleasure at his pupil's progress. 'You be good hunter.'

'I don't think my mother would like that.'

On his next try a strand of elastic came loose from the pouch and snapped back, stinging his outstretched thumb, so they went back into Laki's house for repairs. The bellboy produced scissors and an old motorcycle inner tube from deep within the vine and sat down on the pallet. Jason wondered what else the vine concealed. It was like an open-textured safe, for unless one knew where to thrust one's hands among its leaves and flowers and fruit there would be little chance of finding any particular thing. In response to a patting gesture of the hand he went and sat by Laki, who busied himself trimming a thin length of rubber from the opened-out tube.

'How is your house?' Laki asked as he worked.

'Quite big. Old. We live up a mountain.'

'How many rooms you have?'

'I don't know.' Jason counted to himself. 'Twelve, including the stables downstairs. Oh, thirteen with the bathroom.'

'Thirteen rooms? You have many brothers and sisters? Grandfathers?'

'No, just the three of us.'

'Thirteen rooms and three people?' Laki's estimation of the Hemonys' wealth, which had been slightly dented by the description of the house as 'old', went considerably higher. It would need confirming, however. 'You have TV?'

'We've got one, but sometimes if there's no petrol for the generator it won't work.'

This was inconclusive, although the generator sounded hopeful. 'How many animals?'

'We've got two dogs and four cats. But the cats are nearly wild. They live in the stables.'

'No pigs, cows, goats?'

'Oh, I see. We've got twelve goats and twenty-one sheep.'

Laki looked up. This was a good answer. The richest person in his village had four goats and a huge sow that had to be taken to a neighbour's for mating. One year after a particularly good fishing season when he had lost no nets his father had spent his tiny reserve of cash on a kid which, although it had grown into a plump nanny, proved barren. For a season it had wandered up and down the beach, in and out of the drawn-up boats, browsing on fish entrails and banana peels and whatever daily ration of the villagers' excrement had not already gone to crabs, pigs and dogs. No billy had approached it with more than cousinly interest, so even they had known. In exasperation his father had cut her throat and they and their friends had eaten well for several days. It had always been Laki's dream to have his own goat, let alone a flock of twelve. The twenty-one sheep sounded additionally attractive but to tell the truth he had never seen a sheep and was a little hazy as to what they looked like. He remembered seeing a book once – there had been one at the

elementary school up the coast – and in this book had been
pictures of various animals, some of which he recognised.
He rather thought that sheep had been quite like goats.
Presumably this boy's father would be back in Italy, looking
after them on the mountain. Then he recalled his saying
there were only the three of them. 'Your father is dead?'

'No,' said Jason. 'Not as far as I know. He went off with a
woman.'

'Ah,' said Laki wisely. Where he came from it would have
been thought most dishonourable for a man to desert his
family. By one means or another most men accommodated
themselves, combining fun with honour. Laki presumed
this to be merely a basic living skill for any man, but it was
evidently one this boy's father had not acquired. What a
passive creature his mother must be to have allowed such a
thing, content to accept disgrace for herself and comparative poverty for her children! If she had only taken a
knife to him! But maybe she had. At any rate she did have
golden hair and a kind face as well as smelling nice. The
most extraordinary fantasy came to him then: no, not exactly
a fantasy since that implied a clear imagined picture. This
was more a sense that here a slot opened up, a space into
which somebody might fit himself, though he stopped short
of giving that person either a name or a role. 'You are sad
without father?'

'I don't know. Why, should I be?'

'But mother sad. Very sad and cold at night.'

'My mother's not . . .' began Jason distantly. 'She's a
different sort of person. You'd have to know her to
understand what I mean. She's interested in the Community, in spiritual things, in the Teacher. He's the Swami,
you know.'

'Swami in Italy too you have? Here in Malomba are many
swamis.' But another matter about this peculiar family
urgently needed clearing up. 'Your sister, she is marry?'

'Zoe?' asked Jason in amazement. 'No, she's only just

fifteen. Anyway, I can't imgaine anyone wanting to marry her.'

This news greatly cheered Laki, who had long since stopped cutting rubber. 'Your sister very beautiful girl,' he said fervently. 'She the beautifullest girl I am seeing always.'

'*Zoe* is?' Though, considering it while Laki returned to his snipping, he supposed she might be. It was always so hard to separate how people looked from what one knew about them. Surely when one thought about people it was their words one remembered best, the things they said and the tone they used and the expression in their eyes, not whether their hair was blonde or their tits stuck out. It was especially difficult when talking about a member of the family to say, yes, probably she wasn't bad-looking. Instead he asked, 'Where's your family?'

So Laki told him about the village by the sea in Saramu Province eighty miles away; about the fisherman father, the siblings, his own banishment in order to earn enough to send money home. The bell-boy was not unsubtle; he never mentioned the word 'poor'. Instead he described how when he lived at home his *kancha* had played its part in the family economy, how his skill enabled them to eat morsels of meat.

'Don't you want to go home?' Jason asked.

'Sometimes I go. Very nice place, very quiet. I am happy to seeing my family. But here in Malomba is better. I want to making progress. I' – he lowered his voice and glanced at the closed door – 'I want to leaving this hotel, find better job. But please please, you not tell Mr Muffy.' He just avoided urging the boy to be sure and mention it to his mother. To his slight disappointment Jason swore with great solemnity never to tell a soul. He seemed to relish being given a secret for safe-keeping. 'You and me the same. We both boys long way from home.' A sadness came into his voice. 'But you to going home soon, I guess. You go home very happy. I stay here Malomba very lonely.'

But once more Jason slithered away. 'I don't particularly

want to go home, as it happens. Actually I hate it there. It's so boring. I'm sick of goats and sheep and gurus and *healing*. I want to go to school like the other boys down in the valley. In three years I'll be fifteen. No education, no exam certificates, no job. In Italy they always want to know your school record, even if it's only for a job as a street cleaner. I'll be stuck in Valcognano for the rest of my life making cheese for the Community and getting milk for the groupies who swan in to learn about magic plants and oils and meditation. I'm not allowed one of those,' he flicked at the catapult Laki had nearly mended. 'Mum'd have a fit if I killed anything. Look at all the things you can do. No wonder you're called Lucky.'

Laki, noting the rush and distress of these words while not by any means understanding everything, was not to be outdone.

'But to travelling is good. Very nice, going to everywhere in the world. All my life I am to two places, my home and here.'

'At least you don't have to drag around behind your sister and your mother.'

Jason had lain back on the pallet in exhaustion, blinking at the riven ceiling. In the fragments of blue sky between the vine tendrils he could see the flicker of birds high and far off, swifts dining off the midges carried aloft by the sun's convections.

'How long you stay here?' asked Laki anxiously.

'Oh God, at least until next Thursday. That's when she's seeing this surgeon guy. Her back's bad. Then perhaps he'll need to see her again. We could be stuck here ages.'

The bell-boy was still unclear who 'she' was. The notion of Zoe as a nobly suffering princess was one to which he was increasingly attached. At the moment, though, there was manifest upset closer to hand and the urge to console came over him, for he was a kindly boy. 'I show you things in Malomba,' he promised. 'I show you place to swimming in river, near to town but very clean. Only boys use for swimming. No washing cows or animals.'

'Really?' Jason's voice was still weary but there was interest in it as well. 'What else?'

'One thing I am wanting,' confided Laki recklessly, reclining on an elbow beside him. 'I am always wanting to go inside Lingasumin. Maybe we are trying.'

The name was familiar. 'Isn't that one of the temples closed to visitors?'

'Yes, closed. Very closed. Because they not wanting people to seeing what they do. They doing like this,' and delightedly inserted a brown forefinger into a circle made by the fingers of his left hand.

Jason raised his head. 'Fucking, you mean? Actual screwing?'

'Oh yes. Very many people doing like that together in temple.'

'What, inside a *temple*? I don't believe that.'

But Laki proved a fund of information, quoting all that Mr Tominy Bundash had told him in the kitchen and adding much else besides from his own head. 'They have special medicine to making the man very big,' he finished. Not knowing the word for caterpillar in English, he talked vaguely about secret extracts from plants picked by the light of a new moon. In his experience foreigners like to hear about herbs picked by moonlight. Sometimes they preferred the pickers to be virgins, sometimes wise old hermits, but the moonlight was essential.

'What a strange place Malomba is!' Jason was saying. 'This is the strangest place I've ever been.' For the scent of the vine seemed to have redoubled its strength, the fragments of sky to be infinitely far away and then just inside the ceiling. In the drowsy late afternoon heat the cooing of the pigeons likewise receded and approached. 'A bit like sleepiness, but it's not,' he murmured, stretching.

'*Karesh*,' said Laki knowingly. 'Vine. It makes to sleeping

58

and to waking at same time. We have many stories here about this vine so strong, so power. Many times,' he said, still up on an elbow and dangling the repaired catapult above Jason so that its pouch barely touched his stomach, 'I do like you now. I am lying on bed and looking, only looking at vine. Sometimes I to thinking of everything. Sometimes I to thinking of nothing and sleeping so Mr Muffy ringing the bell and ringing the bell and become very angry to me. Other time I am lying and get very waking, very strong.'

Jason was thrilled by a peculiar pang of being at the centre of something where at last he was not looking on. There was a mesmerism in Laki's hand idly bouncing the pouch on his stomach, then lower down. For the second time that afternoon he found he could not move and wondered vaguely whether the bell-boy would suddenly burst into song. But he didn't. The bouncing rhythm extended itself and began to take in more and more of the room and his eyes gazed past Laki's ear to become snared in the vine's traceries. It was true about Malomba, he thought. It definitely was the strangest place he'd ever been. He kept on falling asleep here. Everything seemed to take place in a dream, while being realer than anything he could re-member. The smell of this vine . . . ! The yellow flowers swelled and glowed as he looked at them, pulsing out their languorous scent. In one corner of his fixed vision the edge of Laki's ear was gently shaking.

On the other side of the vine a pigeon flapped its wings and settled them with a crackle of feathers. Laki, noticing Jason's toes stretching and pointing, stopped. The forgotten catapult's rubber dangled above the white T-shirt. His other fist was resting upright on Jason's bare belly. A band of vine-filtered sunlight fell across it and glinted on the tip of a pale pink nut encircled by his fingers and protruding a scant half inch. Laki looked at it closely, curiously, from across the bewildering territory of difference. Slowly he resumed his movement; the pouch lowered. An immeasurable time passed in which Jason experienced his own fixed gaze, the jiggling ear, the sun-barred vine, the heat and the smell of pigeon-shit and perfume as running into one another, causing the acutest sensations to race and smart through him. By the time Laki's fist had stilled his feet were relaxed and his chest trembled to his heartbeat. The bell-boy was again peering forward as if for information at the pink nut, now barely afloat on a milky rim.

Soon Jason noticed the edge of Laki's ear had started to jiggle again and came up on his elbows to ask, 'What's *sima?*' The ear stopped.

'*Sima,*' said Laki with a sigh. 'Oh, *sima*. Where you hear this name?'

So Jason told him of the torso boy and the handful of brown lumps although without mentioning the singing.

'I know him. That boy is Vippu. Everybody know him. Selling *sima* to tourists. Very bad boy. Sometimes the police they catch and beat to him.'

'They beat a boy with no legs?' cried Jason.

'They beat to everyone,' Laki told him with a certain glee.

'Yes, but what *is* this *sima?*'

'*Sima* is drug. In forest are many magic mushrooms. They are taking and putting in sun like on roof here,' he pointed towards the door, 'so are becoming dry. When become dry they make dust, then take juice of vine fruit and make like this.' He flexed one hand as if moulding a lump of *sima* paste with sticky gourd sap. 'Then it become dry again and are selling. Many tourist to smoking and eating *sima*. Very bad for brains. Very bad drug.'

Jason fell silent thinking about this. Slowly the ear began its jiggling once more. At length he remarked. 'We saw a dog run over by the train in the park today. Mum and Zoe cried.'

This time there was no reply in the little mud room. Attention was narrowing. Whenever either of them swallowed it sounded very loud.

❦

One day a year or so previously, a neatly dressed young man had turned up at Valcognano. His short stay in the Community of Pure Light shed more gloom and caused more upset in that spiritual fastness than Zoe could ever remember.

Ed, an American in his mid-twenties, bore a letter from Swami Bopi Gul himself, writing from Los Angeles on patchouli-scented paper. The letter was brief, extending the Teacher's greetings and blessings to all disciples and beloved friends at his Valcognano temple and introducing Ed as a trusted pupil whose thoughts about the Swami's mission were those of the Teacher himself ... In other words they were to be paid respectful attention.

Once this letter had been read, the simple ceremonies of welcome performed, the phials of oil (blessed by the Swami himself) distributed and meditation held, it quickly became apparent that there was to be a change of policy. Through Ed, the Swami was instructing that more energy be devoted to the growing of medical herbs, the extraction of essential oils and the writing of healing texts. For many years (said Ed) the Valcognano Community had been setting a remarkable example of a way of life full of health and bliss and light, shining out from the Apuan Alps like a spiritual pharos, its harmonious vibrations thrilling through Europe and constituting, however subtly, a force for good. Now it was time to take the Swami's mission a stage further and give his healing secrets wider currency. For the world was sick (Ed said) and getting rapidly sicker. It was polluted by sundry varieties of evil, not least among which were the products of multinational pharmaceutical companies as well as the arrogant pragmatism of Western medicine ...

In short, Valcognano was to go commercial.

Tessa and the other Elders were dumbstruck. Never in the dozen or so years of the Community's existence could they have dreamed of receiving such a message from its

Founder. It seemed a total reversal of his ideas, of everything he had promoted as spiritually beautiful. It caused them an acute crisis of faith. But little by little they argued themselves around, admitting that none of them – for perhaps they *were* a bit unworldly – could presume to question his wisdom nor claim to understand the arcane unknowables which informed his divine guidance. Was the world not changing? And therefore might not a spiritual strategy also need updating in order to remain effective? Under Ed's careful mixture of cajolery and injunction their attitude changed from obstinacy to acquiescence, even enthusiasm.

None of these principled wrestlings made much impact on Zoe. She was alive to the turmoil going on around her but the issues themselves scarcely touched her. It was Ed himself who had the greatest effect on her. The Elders, including her mother, saw him (somewhat jealously) as a messenger, a necessary harbinger. Zoe saw him as very good-looking. He wore tailored tan slacks and an Italian cowboy-boulevardier's shirt in heavy linen. He had a discreet wristwatch and once when he chanced to open his wallet to find an address (a wallet!) she saw a small gold card which said American Express. She had no idea what such appurtenances were, exactly, but what they meant was that Ed was completely different from all the other visitors to Valcognano, and the whiffs of power he exuded were equally of an alien kind.

More marvellous still, he evidently took a real interest in her *as a person* and made a point of asking Zoe herself to guide him round the Community's properties and messuages. Sometimes he held her hand, and she could have fainted with pleasure that this dazzling envoy from another world was treating her not as some grubby peasant girl but as a young lady privy to certain information which he needed.

'Strange horses you have here,' he remarked. 'I thought I knew horseback riding but I've never seen these before.'

'They're not horses,' Zoe told him. 'They're mostly mules.'

'Oh. That thing there's a mule?'

'Well, actually that particular one's a hinny. Mules come from a male donkey mated with an ordinary mare, you know. A hinny's from a female donkey mated with a stallion.'

'My,' said Ed. 'You know a lot.'

'I don't know anything,' cried Zoe, 'not compared with you. There's not much to know here and you soon learn that. But you must know a million things.' She couldn't bring herself to begin listing them. 'And you know the Teacher, too.'

'Sure I know him.' He did not, perhaps, sound quite as overawed as did most people who had experienced the *Presentness* of Swami Bopi Gul; but to Zoe this was merely further proof of Ed's exoticism, of his moving easily and naturally on a rarefied plane. 'And these are the fields where you grow the herbal stuff?'

'These are the Healing Acres, yes.'

'Just this? I wouldn't have said it was even a single acre.'

'We don't need very much.'

'From now on we're going to need a helluva lot more, dear heart.'

Dear heart! 'How much more?'

'We reckon six or eight acres, to start with.'

'Acres? You mean *real* acres?' Zoe thought of all the hours she must have spent since she was old enough to wield a hoe going up and down the three little plots of comfrey, camomile, marjoram, dill, clary sage and so on. Who on earth would have the time to nurse eight acres of herbs?'

'Sure, acres. We're talking expansion. We're talking about injecting some real productivity into this outfit. It's so pretty here: high up, wild, unpolluted. Traditional. Natural.

We can capitalise on all that. Proper packaging, proper labelling. Handwritten guarantees of purity.'

'It doesn't sound . . .' began Zoe doubtfully, '. . . I mean, it doesn't sound quite as *spiritual*, that way.'

A little edge of irritation sharpened Ed's voice. 'Quite as *spiritual*, quite as *spiritual*,' he gently mimicked her English accent. 'It'll be one hundred per cent as spiritual, dear heart. What's the difference? You've always grown comfrey; okay, so now you grow ten times as much fucking comfrey, excuse me, what's the difference? Right, you always pick monk's benison on the night of the new moon. So now you pick a whole lot more monk's benison on the night of the new moon because you've got more fields and more labour. But it's still the right stuff at the right time, isn't it? Nothing faked. No corners cut. You're just upping production, is all. The real thing but more of it.'

There was a pause while Zoe thought about this. 'What's monk's benison?' she enquired timidly. 'I've never heard of that.'

'I just invented it.' A great, intimate, flashing white smile, his beautiful brown hand meanwhile languidly indicating their maize field. 'Anyone ever thought of growing marijuana in the middle of that?'

'I think so. But sometimes the police fly over here in helicopters.'

'Sneaky. It'll just be a matter of finding the right guy to pay so the choppers always check Valcognano out in the winter. I'll get on to that.'

If such remarks brought an alien world closer to the sacred boundaries of the Community, others seemed to consign the Pure Lighters to another place and time.

'My,' he kept saying, not without admiration. 'I guess it's how they used to live in the Sixties. It's kind of quaint to think of those old guys having once been hippies.'

'Those old guys' were Elder Bob and Elder Tessa – her

own mother, in fact, who happened at that moment to be wearing a ratty pair of corduroy trousers and a hat Bruce had left behind. Zoe experienced a pang of pity for her mother, consigned thus to some sociological *oubliette*. Yet somewhere inside her, however unwillingly, Zoe had known Ed was right. There *was* something time-warped about Tessa, about them all. Much as the Pure Lighters kept to themselves—and even when travelling about the world they managed to preserve a *cordon sanitaire* of herbalist naiveté between themselves and whatever they encountered—Zoe had long since deduced that most girls her own age lived very different lives. They knew different things, too, and pursued their interests with what appeared to be scant regard for the opinions of adults and parents. Often when the Hemonys returned to Valcognano they had to change trains in Milan, Bologna or Florence, and having an hour or two to kill would look around town or sit at an open-air café and watch the vivid parade. If the café happened to be in fashion, there would usually be a glittery mass of motor-scooters nearby with youths hitched over black squidgy rubber and chrome talking to girls perched more daintily on chairs at the edge of the pavement. All were dressed like peacocks; the sun shone on combs and teeth and hair and calfskin and rings and studs . . . especially studs.

'Bliss,' her mother would murmur. It did not escape Zoe's attention that many of the boys were rather attractive but she told herself they seemed a bit juvenile (too much laughter, too-casual gestures, too-boisterous hands). She noticed that Tessa's eyes also missed nothing, even as her work-roughened hands spooned ice cream or lifted coffee. It was at such moments that Zoe felt most disloyal. It would, she thought, be quite nice to be preened at by some young man. Every so often a couple would leave and the sudden whizzing and moaning of the little exhausts seemed oddly valedictory and excluding. Where were they off to, leaving her behind in a cloud of sweetish gas with her mother and brother and empty ice-cream cup? All one needed in order to keep cheerful was a bit of attention every now and again. Not necessarily to be praised, nor even to be courted; but for somebody to ask how she felt and acknowledge that she, too, was in the running for . . . for . . . well, for being *considered*.

And now here was Ed who, if ever he had once as a teenager lounged outside cafés, had long since smoothed out and become powerful and was actually asking her to explain things about life in Valcognano. It was beyond daydreams. She thought he could only ever ruin it all by calling her 'kid'; but he never once did, only 'dear heart'.

'You're really something, you know that?' They were drinking fennel tea together in the Swami's house. To Zoe's disappointment, Ed was staying not in her own house but in the one reserved exclusively for the Teacher, sleeping with appalling nonchalance in his actual bed. 'You'd be a sensation in California; they just don't make girls like you any more. Kind of unspoilt, you know? You *are* unspoilt, aren't you, dear heart?'

She had blushed, so unused was she to any kind of notice, still less to compliments, and said she didn't know. According to her impression Ed had found this reply unsatisfactory at the time; but each day for the remainder of his stay he invited her to ramble with him through the chestnut woods and rocky uplands which overhung the village. By the time he came to leave he could doubtless answer his own question. As her mother would later remark, Zoe's heart was warm. She was reduced to sullen misery by Ed's departure, a tragic gloom she nursed for weeks. When the expected letter did not come, not even in answer to several of hers, she began to emerge once more with a passable display of not caring.

And there was plenty going on in the Community to engage interest. Swami Bopi Gul's edicts, as relayed by Ed, were being faithfully carried out. Already Elder Bob, who had once trained as a graphic designer, had sketched out labels and letterheads for Valcognano products. There was a logo and house typography. The logo was a seated Buddha holding a pestle and mortar; the typography a virtuous italic hand. A printer was contacted in Lucca. A small tractor was to be bought from a dealer in Carrara. Curious seeds were written for.

Yet Zoe's interest was not quite engaged. A spell had been broken: that of childhood, maybe, or of authority. Somewhere at the foot of the eight hundred and ninety-four mule steps, down beyond the valley's misty distances, an entire world was busy happening without her. 'You'd be a sensation in California . . .'

Tessa plied her with valerian.

Laki was sitting with Raju on the back doorstep of the kitchen. In one hand he held the clavicle of a monkey from which he every so often sucked shreds of meat and gravy, in the other a letter from home. The letter had been brought by a dried-fish merchant from Saramu Province and left at the hotel desk. It was not easy to decipher, having been written turn and turn about by his mother, his eldest sister and youngest brother Gunath. Reading it was likewise a joint effort. Between them Laki and Raju gathered that his mother had flu and Gunath had shot a *kululu*, the nearly extinct and extravagantly beautiful National Bird which figured so prominently on stamps and coins and banknotes. The *kululu*, known to Europeans as the Rainbow Yodeller, was the size of a large pheasant with long iridescent green tail-feathers. Having been catapulted out of the sky by Laki's brother, it had wound up on a bed of rice dressed in a sauce of unripe guavas and had fed the entire family.

This piece of good news was not, however, the real point

of the letter, which was that the family was suffering hard times. For the past ten days the coastline of Saramu had been afflicted by a Red Tide more sluggish and extensive than any of recent years. This was an intermittent plague in which the sea turned red and soupy and made the fish poisonous to eat; it was apparently caused by a species of plankton which suddenly multiplied hugely; there was nothing to do but wait until the tides and currents had moved it away into the open ocean. Unscrupulous fishermen who could afford ice would send their catches to a distant province where news of the Red Tide had not yet arrived; they could generally dispose of twenty or thirty boxes before the first fatalities. Unscrupulous but poor fishermen without ice contented themselves with expressions of their own virtue. One way or another these tides were a disaster, and Laki's family was not alone in feeling the pinch. Until such time as it was safe to resume fishing, the villagers up and down the coast got by on a diet of boiled cassava and the National Bird.

His mother ended her letter with the hope that life in the big city was pleasurable and profitable. She made no demands for money; she did not need to. Laki had never in his life received a letter which was merely a greeting. All letters were begging letters; that was why people sent them.

'Bad, uncle,' he said, tucking it away and tossing the clavicle to the goat.

'Very bad,' agreed Raju. 'I remember a Red Tide when I was a boy which lasted a whole month.'

Laki wondered how his mother's flu was. There probably wasn't enough spare cash for her to buy her favourite antibiotics in the village shop. At the least sign of indisposition – from headache to arthritis in her ankles – she would go to the shop and search through the big glass sweet-jar containing a ragbag of medicaments. It was not always easy to make a choice because many of the tablets had long since fallen out of their foil wrappers and, grey with handling, were indistinguishable one from another. But his mother was an optimist and had great faith that whatever she selected would work. Her most serendipitous choice to date had been when she put herself on a short course of steroids for toothache and the pain had vanished within minutes. It worried Laki that she might have to face her flu without recourse to the sweet-jar.

'I suppose I could ask Mr Muffy for an advance,' he said without much hope.

'Listen, boy, each time the Muffys of this world pay you at all it's a miracle. To expect them to pay before they have to – a week before, in your case – is like expecting a chicken to fly backwards. They're just not designed for it. You'll have to think of something else.' From the blackened stewpot between them he picked out a tiny wrinkled hand and began nibbling the fingers. 'Far too much cardamom,' he remarked. 'Monkey's a delicate meat; it's wrong to drown it in spices . . . So how are your great plans getting on for leaving this place and becoming Prime Minister?'

'I haven't exactly found anything else yet, uncle, it's true.'

'Ah, but you haven't been wasting your time, have you?' Raju shot him a knowing sideways look. 'Worked your way into any Italian knickers yet, have you?'

'I can't think what you mean,' Laki cried.

'I do beg your pardon. Maybe they're English.' When the boy merely looked confounded the night porter jogged his shoulder. 'I'm not blind,' he said. 'I may be on nights but my eyes and ears still work perfectly well in daylight. "Oho," I say to myself. "Now there's a forward lad showing enterprise beyond the call of his very limited duties, buying fresh *laran* each morning and carrying out structural repairs. But how's he going to turn this beautiful friendship into ready cash?" That's the sort of thing I've been saying to myself.'

This, of course, was the very question uppermost in Laki's mind. With his mother's letter fresh in his pocket the need for cash was acquiring new urgency. And if the session with *hadlam* Tapranne were a success, the Hemonys would not be staying in Malomba much longer. 'There's something about them, uncle,' he said. 'They're different.'

'Really? They seem pretty much the same to me. Quite nice, dim foreigners. But then I've scarcely seen much of them.'

'No, there's something,' insisted Laki. 'It's not just that they're ignorant – all foreigners are ignorant when they come here, aren't they, uncle? Actually, these ones know quite a bit about religion and healing and things. I just think they . . . I think they want something to happen.'

'Well. And what are you talking yourself into, boy?'

'The daughter's very beautiful,' Laki said to the goat as it crunched away. 'Maybe she's the one who's ill. Perhaps she's a . . . a princess in disguise, or something.'

Raju put a finger to one side of the boy's jaw and gently pushed his head into profile against the light from the kitchen. 'No beard,' he said. 'I see no beard. And in any case, what kind of foolishness is this? You don't stand a chance, boy, take it from me. No pretty young European girl is going to look twice at an under-age bell-boy with dark skin in some scruffy provincial hotel. I'm sorry to ruin your dreams, but it's so.' And because Laki looked so crestfallen he added, 'Any more than she'd look at an over-age night porter. They're not here for that sort of thing. The woman's here for psychic surgery. They're serious; they're the wrong sort of people.'

Yet now it was out in the open, even if only to be dismissed, there was something satisfying about hearing it put into words. If the possibility existed as an idea, the possibility existed. Each time he said 'uncle' to Raju, Laki knew he was young and inexperienced, that the milk was still wet on his lips. Yet for the first time he had had an intuition he could not easily dismiss. He still thought the Hemonys were people who wanted something to happen and that there must be a way of converting this unfocused desire into advantage, into preferment, into cash. The heretical notion crossed his mind that the venerable Raju might be wrong; that anything could be made to happen with anyone, foreign or not. And chasing this idea came another, glimpsed in triumphant outline against an inner skyline: if Raju were so wise, why was he still a night porter at fifty-six?

He made his way up the back stairs, stopping at Zoe's floor to walk softly along the passageway and pause outside her door. Not a sound came from within, nor any light from crack or keyhole. Laki pictured her lying on her bed in an attitude of the utmost chastity, dressed in a voluminous white silk nightgown and with her blonde tresses spread on her pillow, a vision drawn largely from the film *Sleeping Beauty* which had recently been playing in town. Sadly he tiptoed away and paused on the floor above outside her brother's door. But again there was no sign of life within and he recalled it was only nine o'clock in the evening and the family was doubtless dining out.

He went on up to the roof and, catapult in hand, sat on the edge beneath the hanging brow of vine to gaze out across Malomba as if for inspiration. The holy city was quite as impressive at night as by day. There were lights everywhere. The shops remained open until late and a thousand bulbs, pressure lamps, candles and kerosene flares poured their luminance from doorway and window, from booth and bazaar. Spires and temples were outlined with strings of coloured lights. A madonna with a faulty neon halo winked coquettishly from above the façade of the pro-cathedral. Chinatown was a mass of green and red strip lighting. In the centre of town it seemed that only the Glass Minaret was unlit: not for the Ibn Ballur mosque the vulgar displays of artifice. Its great architect had planned that only the pure radiance of stars and moon would dash itself against his vision into seven hundred and seventy-seven thousand fragments. Unfortunately he had not foreseen twentieth-century technology. For hundreds of years his minaret had

71

glittered austerely to the lunar phases like a column of mercury droplets stilled. Nowadays, though, its lower facets gave off haphazard sparks of pink neon, crude limes and raw oranges, as if at last an acidic pollution were seeping upwards from its base.

Near the Chinatown gateway Laki could pick out a single point of deep ruby. This was the glans of the phallus atop the Lingasumin, otherwise an unlit squat bulk full of suggestive possibilities. At night his eyes were drawn to it as much as his feet by day. How was he ever to get a glimpse inside? Given the intimate and restricted nature of the congregation, it was surely impossible to infiltrate it in disguise, particularly as sooner or later every last stitch would have to be removed. A simple turban would clearly not suffice. In any case the only people he had ever seen going into the Lingasumin had been dressed as ordinary businessmen in shiny Indian suits, some carrying small fibre suitcases about whose contents he could only speculate.

How anguishing it was to be so full of pressing needs of one sort or another while having to sit and stare out over a city crammed with potential! Nobody understood a boy's dilemma, Laki thought, least of all old people like Raju. To be full of energy and yet to be constantly frustrated! Thanks to friends like Mr Bundash, he understood much of what went on in Malomba; yet whenever he sat beneath his vine and breathed its perfume, his mind seemed to drowse and skid off among possible projects as numerous as the streets and alleys below him which fumed them up. His mother, now: he really had to get some money to the family within the week. But how? Theft? That was the most obviously straightforward way of getting things in this world, but Laki had witnessed the public flogging in the market-place of many thieves, real or alleged, and it was not a risk he cared to run. The last victim had expired of heart failure beneath the rod, for all that a sympathetic crowd had exercised its prerogative of pelting his lacerated buttocks with rotten fruit in between strokes in order to soothe and cool them. So if not theft, what? Wherein lay money?

The answer staring him in the face was, of course, religion. It was Malomba's number one industry and, despite Raju's warning, he still thought it had possibilities. For twenty minutes or so he turned over various ideas for founding a religion. Most of them quickly degenerated into outlines of rites involving virgins and several times he had to force himself back on to strictly practical lines of thought. Probably the best plan would be to found one with a few friends and build some kind of simple chapel somewhere. Then they would be added to Malomba's list as its fortieth temple. They could charge admission to tourists and visiting anthropologists and give expensive interviews for their hand-held videos. Laki began to warm to his idea. They would need a unique selling point: a new kind of deity, certainly, since the old ones were all spoken for; or a system of worship so arcane that people would pay or do anything to watch it. (The ruby light glowed steadily some way off below him.)

No, that was too unoriginal. He could never hope to beat the Left-Handed Shaktas at that game. All right then, what about something so flamboyant it was a spectacle no one would want to miss? But the trouble with robes and lace and cloths of gold was that they were hopelessly outside his budget. Maybe he ought to settle for building up a reputation as a very *spiritual* sect. Laki was not at all sure what this meant, but he had heard it said that a people's true spirituality could be measured by the austerity of their worship, and wasn't austerity another word for cheapness? For example, he had also heard it said that the Chinese were the least spiritual people in town, and certainly the carryings-on in their quarter seemed to bear this out. They were forever holding dragon parades with all manner of fireworks and colourful bedlam which obviously cost a fortune. Then at night the narrow streets of Chinatown

73

echoed to the crash and the rattle of mah-jongg tiles in upper rooms where slow-bladed fans stirred thick air beneath the actinic glare of strip lighting. Rumour had it that still further fortunes were nightly won and lost. Terrible fights broke out, and he remembered once seeing somebody's entrails hanging from a window-box. Worship of any kind seemed to have slipped unnoticed from the Chinese calendar, squeezed out by a busy round of festivals, opening new hotels, moneymaking and the more fanciful kinds of divination.

At the opposite extreme, Laki guessed, lay something called Anglicanism, whose adherents were so austere and restrained their church had stood completely unattended for thirty-one years. Mr Bundash was his only source of information about this religion, since the building itself had been pulled down well before he arrived in Malomba. It was indeed the only example of a religious edifice so redundant as to have merited demolition. On its site now stood the Vudusumin from which screaming could occasionally be heard.

Laki presumed that ranking next in austerity to this defunct church was the grey stone building on the outskirts of town known as the Auld Strait Kirk. This was something of a memorial to a small band of Scotsmen who had come to the area in the last century to start the tea plantations with which they intended to rival Ceylon. They had not easily relinquished this plan. One by one they were carried off by disease, drink and despair, but not before they had built a church to invoke God's blessing on their enterprise and his mercy on their souls. Scotsmen had long since died out in Malomba, but the church was still patronised by a handful of locals led by their Elder, Hamish Patel. Laki had once passed the open door during a service and had glimpsed a bare room with a tableful of hats and people chanting lugubriously. One could hardly get more austere than that, he decided; and since that moment this church had come to represent for him the apogee of spirituality.

Thus as he sat beneath the heavy-scented vine he sketched out the Auld Strait Kirk of Laki, Malomban Rite, whose temple was a building bare of all needless extravagance but for a plain table piled high with virgins . . . No, he thought crossly, trying to shake the drowsiness out of his head, he would have to do better than this if he were to be sending money home this week. He got to his feet and moodily kicked a chunk of mud brick from the dovecote wall, loosing part of it into the Redemptorist Fathers' garden with his catapult. The garden lay in total darkness but for swarms of fireflies, and it gave him satisfaction to hear the dried mud smack against the invisible pagoda, which was what he had been aiming for.

On impulse he thrust the catapult away and hurried downstairs. Behind the desk in the hall Raju sat staring glassily at a picture of a paddy field on the opposite wall. The picture concealed a hole caused by Mr Muffy's attempt to put up a fusebox which had been mysteriously stolen before it could be screwed in place. Laki recognised the porter's glassiness as authentically that induced by palm toddy, a flagon of which would be set down out of sight by his feet.

'Are they in, uncle?' he asked.

'Who, boy?'

'Those foreigners. You know.'

'Ah. Er,' Raju twisted his head and squinted up at the board, 'no, doesn't look as if they are. The keys are all here. And no, you can't have the pass-key.'

'I don't want it,' Laki told him with virtuous surprise. 'Why would I?'

'If Muffy ever found I'd given you the key so you could go skulking about guests' rooms after dark, it'd be as much as my job's worth. You'd lose yours, too, but not before you'd also lost a few inches of skin off that handsome little backside.'

How dreadfully drunk he is tonight, thought Laki as he went upstairs once more. He passed through to the servants' staircase and sat down on the dusty brick landing which led to Mrs Hemony's corridor, turning off the light and slightly opening the door so he might hear her approach. He had scarcely begun to doze before he heard the sound of voices and feet on the marble steps. To his relief the two children went straight up to their rooms after mutual good nights, leaving their mother to make her way slowly along in the gloom to her own door. Just as she reached it Laki produced a handkerchief and, pressing it to his face, stumbled through the landing door towards her as his other hand groped for the switch. The light came on and, catching sight of her, he affected to pull himself together.

'Good evening, missus,' he said thickly.

'Lucky! Why, whatever is the matter?' Tessa paused in the act of unlocking.

'Oh, missus. Oh, it is nothing.'

'Are you hurt, then? Ill?' She withdrew the key and pushed the door, reaching round its edge to turn on her own light.

'No, not ill, missus. Not sick. Oh!'

'Then what? You can tell me, Lucky. We're friends, aren't we?' She put a maternal hand on his shoulder and drew the overcome bell-boy into her room. 'Maybe I can help.'

Laki was shaking his head and sniffing. 'No, missus, you very kind. Everyone say how kind the missus. But no help can give. It my mother. Oh!'

'Your mother? She isn't dead?'

A wail, bravely stifled, escaped the handkerchief. 'Not dead, missus. Or maybe now she dead.' From his pocket he drew the letter and gave it to Tessa.

'Oh dear, oh dear, Lucky, I can't read your language.' She turned the grimy sheet over and over as if looking for familiar roman letters among the elegant curlicues of the script.

'It from my brother. He say' – Laki took back the letter

and skimmed it distractedly as if searching for a single recognisable word amongst the illiterate scrawl – 'he say here my mother very very sick to Red Fever.'

'Red Fever? *Scarlet* fever? Oh Lucky, how awful! I'm truly sorry. When was the letter sent?'

'One week. Oh.'

'She's at home in your village?'

'Yes, yes. Saramu Province. Very far, very poor. I am thinking she to dying without medicine.'

'Well,' said Tessa, being practical, 'first you must telephone to find out how she is.'

'Oh missus, no telephone. No telephone arriving in Saramu.'

'What, none in the entire province?'

'No telephone, missus. I think she to needing medicine not telephone. But no have money. How much they pay me here to Nirbana Hotel is nothing. Oh.'

'I see.' As indeed she did, being suddenly reconciled to funding his poor mother's recovery. 'How far away is this village of yours?'

'Eighty miles, missus.' The alarming thought struck him that she might insist on going in person. 'Very bad bus. Very danger road because of freedom fighters. Bandits, they kill. Also Saramu Province close now.'

'The province is closed?'

'Yes, yes, closed. No are going. Policemen to stopping. Too much bandit. Too much Red Fever.'

'Poor Lucky.' Tessa was visualising his mother lying sick in a rude hut on a remote littoral isolated by indigence, guerrilla activity and contagious disease, and was not stuck for a remedy. 'Pennyroyal,' she said. 'We must see how we can get her some oil of pennyroyal at once. Is she pregnant? I mean, she's not having a baby?'

'No, no, my father he tie.'

This syntax made her unwilling to pursue the subject further. 'In that case she can have pennyroyal. It's wonderful for the kidneys and that's where the danger lies in scarlet fever. Oh, and cypress oil.'

'I think she wanting antibiotic, missus.'

Poor child (thought Tessa); I haven't the heart to explain the dangers of conventional medicine to him at this moment. As soon as the crisis was over, though, she resolved to set him straight. But first things first. His evident upset must be calmed since the bond between mother and son was such that if his spirit were distraught it might materially affect her chances of recovery. This was one of the Swami's greatest Teachings, that mental distress produced far worse imbalances than any physical yin-yang disequilibrium. She sat Laki down on the edge of her bed, where he perched with the unease of a child who knows himself to be out of bounds even though in extenuating circumstances. 'Now look,' she took one of his hands. 'Your mother will be all right. *I know*. She will be well, do you understand? We'll send her antibiotics.'

'Oh missus, you kind kind lady. But it better we send money for to buy.'

'But can she get antibiotics where she is?'

'Yes, yes, village shop they have.'

'Antibiotics in a village shop?' Even in a country as bizarre as this it seemed unlikely.

'Yes, yes. But very expensive, missus.'

Well, she supposed they would be. 'How much do you need, Lucky?'

'Oh missus, too much . . . You too kind . . . No, no. Oh.' This babbling, during which he blotted his eyes once more, gave him the chance to think for a moment. What was it reasonable to ask for? He had been resigned to getting Raju to lend him a twenty-note under the veiled threat of reneging on his part in the toddy-tapping. In the best of all possible worlds – that obtaining within minutes of getting his salary on time from Mr Muffy – he might have aspired to fifty *piku*. How high would she go? 'A hundred is . . .' He choked tactically.

'Of course, Lucky.'

'. . . not enough, missus. I think maybe two hundred okay. But you must not to giving me. I am nothing. I am unknown boy.' And he dabbed afresh.

But Tessa was taking four fifty-notes from her purse. 'Don't be silly, Lucky, you're our friend. You've helped us and now we're doing a bit in return. Even if you were a complete stranger it's bliss to be able to help people, isn't it? Now look.' She folded up the notes and tucked them into the pocket of his jacket. 'You go right off and send your mother what she needs with our love and tell her she's already getting better. All right?' And she patted the back of his hand encouragingly.

Laki grasped her fingers and impulsively drew them to his lips. By now he firmly believed his mother's life had been saved and real tears stood in his eyes. 'Oh missus, missus, you too too kind for me. I always be your friend. I always be your bell-boy.'

'Why, Lucky.' Tessa sat next to him with her hand imprisoned at his mouth, somewhat embarrassed by the effusiveness, the absurdity of the situation, the disparity between them. But even as she blushed she was conscious of their proximity and above all the elusive scent his clothing gave off, some kind of exotic flower maybe. At that instant he looked up at her from beneath long, tear-fringed lashes and met her gaze with something besides dumb gratitude. 'How silly,' she heard herself say. 'Of course we shall always be friends. But you won't always be my bell-boy. Or any kind of boy,' she added. One of her hands detached itself of its own accord from his mouth and, with the halting delicacy of a butterfly, alighted for the briefest moment before fluttering away to rest in her own lap. 'Goodness,' she breathed. 'Come along then.' She stood up purposefully but carefully in case her back were suddenly painful. 'Off you go. The sooner your mother gets the medicine the sooner she'll get well. But come back sometime and I'll show you

how to heal a person at a distance. If I knew you better and
we'd had a chance to get on the same spiritual wavelength, I
could have helped to heal your mother through you, right
here in this very room. But first I'd need to get a special oil
and do some reflexology on you.'

Laki, having pulled his jacket down as far as it would go,
got awkwardly to his feet and made for the door. 'Thank
you, missus,' he said huskily. 'One day I to showing you my
room. Very beautiful the vine there. You will come see?'

'I promise,' said Tessa. 'Good night.'

'Good night, my missus. Oh.'

He went softly away up the corridor. Once through the
door on to the brick landing he gave a little skip and raced
lightly upstairs to his den. From the depths of the vine he
dug out one of the hotel's smudgily-printed envelopes,
addressed it to home, scrawled a brief message and
enclosed a fifty-note. The other three notes he thrust into
the bowels of the plant before trotting downstairs and out
into the street in search of the dried-fish merchant. All
within an hour his fortunes had changed and things were
looking up. Now anything was possible. As he passed the
Lingasumin, its glowing ruby rekindled the embers of a
considerable ardour he had felt at the end of his visit to the
missus. He was right; these people really did want something to happen.

❧✿❧

When the pain in her back became intractable enough to
make her plan this trip, Tessa had spoken to Swami Bopi
Gul on the telephone. This instrument was screwed to a
wall in the bar below Valcognano, and allowing for the
transatlantic time difference she usually found herself
making such calls in the evening against the din of card

games and television. The Teacher was not an easy man to speak to; generally she got through to Ed, who would then vanish off the line in search of him. A fifteen-minute wait was not uncommon, during which the little counter behind the bar clocked up the *scatti* at an alarming rate. It had never occurred to Tessa to mention this. One did not trouble swamis with such trivia, still less did one ask an incarnate god to accept reverse-charge calls.

On this occasion he had been quite prompt and within seven minutes was saying, 'Of course, my dear Tessa, you absolutely must go to Malomba. There are wonderful things in that place. It will be arranged for you to see *hadlam* Tapranne, a great and good healer who is close to us. While you are there—'

A deafening burst of cheering from behind her blotted out the Teacher's gentle tones. Someone had scored a goal on television.

'— many new essences for Pure Light Products, maybe. You understand, my dear, this has never been done before. Is it not exciting? To this person it is the greatest bliss to know that at last a serious effort is being made to coordinate the world's most potent healing substances in order to attack the modern evils. The work of our movement is to become a united healing agency, able to supply any essence from anywhere, able to use any of the sacred techniques the ancients practised and which have been temporarily – temporarily, mind – smothered by the three modern evils.'

'Technology. Speed. Mass media.'

'Technology. Speed. Mass media,' echoed the Swami from seven-odd thousand miles away. 'Exactly. But then you are one of our oldest and dearest disciples, even though I know you have been a little troubled.'

'Master, I am in bliss.'

'Of course. But we *know*, my dear. We *know* you did not at first understand our plan when Ed came and explained it to you. Come now, you were troubled.' The Swami's delicious laugh sounded down the wire.

81

'Perhaps just for an instant, Master. It was stupid of me.'

'But now you perceive?'

'With all my heart, Teacher.' For she really did. To combat the degeneration of human spiritual life on this planet, one needed to borrow certain leaves from the book of so-called Progress. *Turn their weapons on themselves, but with love.*

'Good. So turn their weapons on themselves, but with love. Organise. Be efficient . . . And how is your delightful family? Ed tells me your daughter is becoming truly beautiful. He describes her as a creature of the most delicate light. I am now wondering whether she ought not to come to California. She—'

Another goal was scored. Someone knocked a metal chair to the marble floor. When the noise had diminished Tessa discovered Swami Bopi Gul had gone, and all she could hear was an expensive electrical hum as she clamped the receiver to her head.

This conversation explained why some weeks later in Malomba she took Laki's advice and engaged Mr Tominy Bundash, official guide, to help her track down a good local source of natural medicine. Zoe decided to accompany her. Before they left the hotel that morning Tessa had a brief, confidential word with Mr Muffy.

'I want you to do something for me,' she said. 'A simple act of kindness. My son Jason wants to go swimming and your bell-boy Lucky has very sweetly offered to take him somewhere he knows where boys go. I'd like you to lend us Lucky for a bit – on a sort of half-day, you know? He's been most considerate to us.'

Mr Muffy, who had initially faced her with an expression of benign accommodation, began to exhibit signs of incredulity.

'Considerate, madam? Laki? Half-day?'

'Come on, why not? I presume you're obliged by law to give all your employees time off? Especially child employees,' she added with what she imagined was a hint of the official reprisals which could always be called down. But the proprietor was still shaking his head.

'Here in Malomba, madam, it is not customarily to giving bell-boys half-days off. They are at the onset of their careers when they must acquire the correct attitude to work which will see them through the rest of their lives. One cannot begin by giving them holidays. Laki has duties.'

Tessa glanced pointedly at the board behind his head. A key hung from nearly every hook.

'I'm sure he has duties. But I'm asking this as a favour and not just for my own convenience, either. The fact is' – she leaned forward and lowered her voice – 'the poor boy's most upset about his mother.'

'His mother?'

'Yes. I'm sure he won't have told you, but she's actually very ill with scarlet fever. She's going to be all right, though.'

'Scarlet fever?'

At this moment Jason and Laki appeared. Mr Muffy gave his bell-boy a look and thought he had never seen anyone less upset. In the circumstances, however, a group of foreign guests leaning on his desk constituted *force majeure*, so he contented himself with a resigned nod.

'You're a truly kind man,' Tessa told him. Zoe shot him a brilliant smile which produced a watery sensation in his stomach and practically reconciled him on the spot to this unheard-of arrangement. She really was, Mr Muffy thought, at the most perfect moment of ripeness. She was like a farewell-fruit as it acquired its rich colours of dusk but before it attained its squashy midnight purple . . . Without visualising anything definite he experienced the psychic sensation of *biting*, of a soft and sweet firmness around his mouth parts which were not located on his face, particularly, but over his whole body. The farewell-fruit, delicious and dangerous . . . To think of that ragamuffin creeping his way into such company! He directed a stony glare at Laki's back as the boys went out. Scarlet fever? What nonsense had the little rogue been selling them? There were things here which needed investigation.

Mr Bundash, special guide, was at his best this morning. Tessa explained what she and Zoe were interested in finding, and when he had listened gravely he announced an itinerary.

'It is evident that a certain quarter of the Wednesday Market shall be our destination. Our way will take us past the celebrated Temple of Ashes. You have visited this yet, madams?'

'I've lost count,' said Zoe.

'I think we haven't,' Tessa told her. 'I believe it's the only major one we've not yet seen.'

The Temple of Ashes was certainly eye-catching from the outside, being shaped more or less like a huge marble wigwam. It was regularly rubbed with cinnabar and it burned at the junction of two streets, a silent stone bonfire. The inside was as unrelievedly grey as the outside was vermilion. Light – and, during the monsoon, rain – came from a circular opening at its apex and fell on the Burning Floor immediately beneath. The sound of their feet was muffled by grey powder which puffed greasily about their ankles as they entered.

'This,' said Mr Bundash in a reverently hushed voice, 'is the world's foremost centre of Spodist worship. It may be that you are not fully conversant with the history of Spodism, so I will recount it briefly. It is believed to have had its origin in Asia Minor some two thousand years before the birth of the Holy Prophet Mohammed, probably as a reaction against the relentless symbolisation of spring, rebirth and fertility as commonly celebrated by cults such as Adonis-Tammuz and the Canaanite Ras Shamra ritualism. The name, of course, is of Greek origin, from the word *spodos*, ashes. I'm not going too fast for you, madams? No, excellent.

84

'Veiled in obscurity as it is for us – although the Spodist priesthood has its own somewhat tendentious account – this religion must certainly predate Zoroastrianism in what is now Iran. One uses the expression "religion" loosely, perhaps. It is more of a philosophy since there is no real deity. Scholars nowadays consider it was this very lack which made inevitable Zarathustra's reforms as well as his widespread acceptance as Servant of the Supreme Wise Lord, Ahura Mazda. We might also agree,' said Mr Bundash, glancing cautiously around. 'that the Spodists' belief was too fatalistic, too bleak for mass appeal.

'Now follow me closely here, madams. For them the supreme principle of the universe is what modern science refers to as *entropy*, which is the innate tendency of things to become disordered, to incline towards their own destruction as discrete systems. Thus the only abiding thing is fire. The ancient Spodists looked into the skies of Asia Minor and saw fire: the relentless sun by day, the unchanging stars by night.' He lowered his voice once more. 'Naturally, they did not have the benefit of telescopes so they could not know that many of the stars they saw were not on fire at all but dead and freezing and merely reflecting light, like our moon. Nor could they have known that even our sun is steadily being consumed.'

'O naïve, naïve Bundash.' A soft but penetrating voice came from a dim grey boulder rolled against one wall and now slowly getting to its feet.

Mr Tominy Bundash clutched at his chest. 'Your forgiveness, reverend sir,' he said. 'I had not realised you . . . I mean . . .'

'O Bundash, how many times have I heard you in this our temple giving your account of our beliefs? You think you are not heard, but I tell you the least whisper carries. I believe,' he added in a mischievous imitation of the guide's voice, 'I believe it is what modern science refers to as *acoustics*.'

'Oh dear, oh dear,' said Mr Bundash unhappily. This was

terrible; if there were a complaint by any of Malomba's religious he could well lose his official status and with it his ID card in its leather wallet. 'Oh, dear me.'

'It's the fault of the system, madams.' The High Priest was addressing Tessa and Zoe as he advanced genially with little puffs of dust. 'It's one of the inherent ironies of mass tourism which has Moslems explaining Spodism to Christians, to say nothing of philistines lecturing the indifferent about masterpieces of art and architecture. But I would not dignify this irony with the name of entropy. No; I would simply call it *Bundashism* and leave it at that.'

'I say, I say,' protested Tominy Bundash. Tessa smiled at him and took his hand sympathetically.

'Actually, we aren't Christians,' she said.

'I have an appointment, madam,' said the High Priest, pulling back his ragged grey vestments to glance at his watch. 'Otherwise I should be delighted to set the record straight at some length. But I cannot go without correcting your guide's naïve misapprehension. It is not of the least consequence whether we know or do not know that the sun is being consumed. Neither telescopes nor any other instrument can weaken or enhance the Spodist position. We are not talking about literal fire, you understand, but metaphorical fire. It is the Incandescence in whose midst we are nothing, and with us the world, the solar system and the universe. It is the same all-consuming Incandescence which can be found blazing at the heart of a sun and in the entrails of a corpse. We do not worship it but the *thought of It*. That is all. The good man is he who contemplates not the fire but its ashes. And so each year we make a model of the world and burn it here on the Burning Floor. It is a symbolic act. Otherwise the Burning Floor is used only for Spodists themselves, many of whom are sent thousands of miles from their native lands for incineration in this our holiest shrine.'

'When . . . when they're dead?' asked Zoe nervously.

'Of course when they're dead, young madam,' said the

High Priest with an air of magnificent patience. 'Do you take us for barbarians? For them it is the final honour to lie here. Who dares walk on dust and not know himself dust?' His voice had taken on the plummy richness of somebody quoting scripture. 'For all seeing is this: that the flame which will consume us was lit at the moment of our birth. Now I must be going.' And with a slight bow he made off, trailing clouds.

'You don't think . . . ?' said Zoe presently, scuffing the toe of a sandal.

'Oh yes,' said Mr Bundash, following her gaze. 'I was coming to that. We are of course walking on his congregation.'

They left and headed for the Wednesday Market. On the way Mr Bundash regained some of his self-confidence; it was evident he was grateful for Tessa's reassurances that his was indeed a difficult job involving feats of memory and discretion. How could anyone reasonable expect a guide to get the most finicking points of doctrine correct in all thirty-nine of Malomba's temples?

'Yes, yes, madam, you perfectly understand. Exactly. I am a good Moslem and yet I tell you in strictest confidence' – glancing round for a disguised imam – 'sometimes I almost begin to forget the tenets of my own faith. It was worse still when there were more tourists here. I would go to bed at night with my head full of texts and think how beautiful these scriptures often were, how like poetry in their truthfulness. Then with a horror I would sit up on my bed because I realised they were not always from the Holy Qu'ran at all but from a dozen infidel books. Oh yes indeed, they were from the Sayings of Rimmon or the Book of Mormon or the Vedas or the Testament of Wisdom. They were from the Talmud or the Torah or the Kabbalah. They were from the Bible or the Book of Splendour, the Revelations of Mithras, the Sublime Recipe, the Analects of Confucius, the Bhagavad-Gita and on and on until my head was whirling with noble truths instead of allowing me to go to sleep and rest my tired feet.

'I was no longer certain even of who I was, madams. My dear wives would say, "Tominy-*da*, Tominy-*da*, what are you becoming? This is not the good Moslem gentleman we married." It was my head, you see. Can you believe it was bursting with commandments, edicts, laws, injunctions and precepts? Oh yes. *Do this. Don't do that. Never do the other except on the last Thursday in the month when there is no menstruating woman in the house.* I wish I had a fifty-note for every Last Judgement which I've been obliged to attend in my nightmares, madams. Oh, it is grisly. Over and over again the universe destroyed in various ways: floods, plague, holocaust, nuclear war. And over and over again this poor Bundash condemned to burn for ever, to drown for ever, to lie in a tent eating dates for ever. Oh, he is beaten and winnowed and flayed and broken on wheels. And once, madams,' their guide gave a mildly crazed laugh, 'I awoke screaming because an archangel was to give me enemas of chillies for the rest of eternity. But I see we've arrived now.'

For they had reached the Wednesday Market and began to wind in and out of alleys crowded with people and merchandise of every variety. All at once Zoe spied a heap of fruit like spiked grenades inside a padlocked wire cage. In response to her query they stopped.

'Those are the famous farewell-fruit,' Mr Bundash said. 'I'm most happy you should have seen them. It's a lucky chance, since their supply is irregular.'

'But why are they locked up?'

'To prevent theft, young madam. Heavens, they are costly. Each one is worth' – he did a sum on his fingers – 'approximately seventeen American dollars. That's more than the poorest of Malomba's poor can expect in one month.'

'They're a little like midget durians.' Tessa bent to sniff the cage. 'Only they don't smell as bad.'

The owner of the stall was looking on with the indifference of one who has seen many tourists stop and very few buy. Mechanically he took two flimsy yellow leaflets from a flyblown stack and handed one each to Tessa and Zoe. They read them while Tominy Bundash gave his own explanation, and from these two sources learned something of why this fruit was so highly prized.

Apparently the local name translated as 'good night', for when fully ripe they were the purple of a tropic dusk. The name had a jocular import, too, for the fruit's many matchhead-sized seeds were violently poisonous and, coated as they were with jelly, slipped down all too easily with the flesh.

This flesh was indeed unimpressive-looking, with something of the bland appearance of tinned pears; but in trying to describe its flavour one approached the farewell-fruit's central mystery. This was, that it had no flavour whatsover – or at least, no two people could agree on it. Each tasted something different and only the most prosaic (such as writers of travel guides and cookery books) tried likening it to the marriage of a strawberry and a cherry, or passion-fruit with overtones of peach.

Generations of writers and travellers, among them Lafcadio Hearn, had left accounts of the glories of this fruit, often reaching modest heights of lyricism. But according to many thoughtful gastronomes the most accurate description of all was by the National Poet, Bard-Professor Stiftu. In one of his *Essays of a Hermit* he had written:

> To eat a farewell-fruit is to leap willingly into the ambush of one's past. For the taste is of childhood, of our private history; and that is why it cannot be compared to any other thing. Children don't like it because to them it is without flavour, even nauseating. It is an adult taste and as we grow older the search [for it] takes on more and more the nature of a risky pilgrimage ... In each fruit are tears and laughter, light and

shade, the energy of sunlight and tropical ennui. And always behind it the threat of death: the golden pips which bring oblivion.

This fanciful exposition was not, according to the pamphlet, to everybody's taste, any more than the fruit itself. It seemed that while they were listening to their guide and reading these leaflets they had been carried along by the flow of people and were now far away from the stall. They found themselves in an alley hung with low awnings which nearly met in the middle. Tessa and Zoe were made suddenly aware of how much taller they were than most Malombans. They stooped beneath these tarry baldachins and drew into their lungs a boiling reek of spice and aromatics.

'Cinnamon, cloves, cardamom,' Tessa began listing appreciatively. 'We must be getting close.'

'Yes, madam,' Tominy Bundash called back, 'we have entered the spice markets. And this' – he dived down a passage – 'is the street of essences.' His voice hung in the air like dust and when Tessa and Zoe turned the corner he was at first nowhere to be seen. They were in a tiny lane lined with dark booths from whose depths rolled perfumes to make their heads swim. The heat was immense, and into it distillates and vapours leached and seeped from a thousand vials and jars, bundles of herbs and thuriferous twigs. A brace of dried bats hung from a string in one doorway, a plywood tub of smoked sea-horses stood in another. Within each hovel they glimpsed shelving with rows of bottles in which sullen oils smouldered. 'Here, here, madams,' and following the voice they came on their guide inside one of these stores talking to a plump oriental wearing what looked like a melted fez whose limp felt ballooned slightly above his ears.

'Come in, come in, ladies!' cried this man in a high voice. 'I am Mr Mokpin. Ong Mokpin of Divine Essence at your services.'

He seated them hospitably on two upturned barrels

cushioned with squabs made of beige and stuffed with hay. Mr Bundash perched behind them on a sack.

'Oh deary me, this heat,' said Mr Mokpin. 'First, refreshment.' He tinkled a bell and a child ran up with a brass tray in one hand and a circlet of straw in the other. 'No,' he said to his guests, holding up his hand although neither had made to speak, 'permit me to order. I can see right away that we wouldn't be content with the usual gassy rubbish. Mops and Bolly and Coca-Cola are not for us. An infusion, perhaps? Something cooling to clear both brow and blood? I'm wondering about a blend of tansy and mulva flowers, but even as I wonder I'm thinking no, our guests are maybe still unused to our homeothermal practice of cooling ourselves with hot drinks. Ah, I have it.' He addressed the child in a few abrupt phrases and it vanished.

Tessa, already excited by Mr Mokpin's herbal precision, spent the short interim looking about her at his shop. The proprietor followed her evident interest with a smile of pleasure. As her eyes adjusted to the gloom, she thought she had never seen so many bottles. The shelves around the walls supported a positive library of oils and essences. Zoe meanwhile was examining a glass jar which held what looked like small lumps of rock under an inch or two of yellowish oil.

'What are these?' she asked.

'Those, young lady, are bezoar. Do you know what bezoar is? No? It's a stone which forms in the stomach of a goat. Ground up, it's a wonderful antidote to all kinds of poison. I can tell you that in the old days the kings of this country always carried a few grains of bezoar powder in the gold heads of their wands of office and never went anywhere without them. Of course we're talking of a period in our history which was very troublous and marked by assassinations and conspiracies of all kinds. I doubt if our beloved present King bothers taking bezoar about with him, but here in Malomba there are those who still swear by it. Ah!'

This interjection signalled the return of the child, brass

tray balanced on the little circlet of straw on his head. The tray held four glasses and a tin pitcher. Ong Mokpin gave him some coins and he scampered off. Then he poured a light blue liquid into each glass, watching the expression on his guests' faces with some amusement.

'Now, ladies, tell me the truth. You'd never seen a blue drink before, no? We call it *masan-masan*, which means "quick-quick", because it acts so fast. Thirst simply melts away.' He sipped at his own glass as if to reassure them.

The liquid, although cool, was by no means chilled; yet its effect was to produce a pleasant freezing sensation in the mouth which at once spread to all parts of the body.

'It's a mixture,' said Mr Mokpin to forestall the obvious question. 'It's basically juice from the flowers of our belfry palm which you may have seen. Heavy clusters of violet bells? Those ones. Although in fact the blue colour of *masan-masan* comes from the empyrean crocus which grows in our forests here. You like it? You're contented?'

'We're in bliss,' Tessa told him happily. 'It's quite delicious.' She turned and smiled at Mr Bundash on his sack, so that mournful gentleman should not feel forgotten. 'I'm more than ever grateful to our friend for bringing us here. Otherwise we would never have found it.'

'I doubt that, Mrs Hemony. Sooner or later the right people usually seem to end up at Divine Essence.'

She was at first disconcerted by his casual use of her name. That quizzical gaze from beneath the doughy fez irritated her fleetingly. 'Oh, I suppose our guide must have told you just now who we were.'

'On the contrary. If I remember rightly, he said, "I've brought you some visitors of remunerative possibility, respected Ong." Mr Bundash habitually talks like that because he's a Moslem. I'm afraid I tend to be more brisk because I'm a businessman . . . No, I knew who you were because of course I had received a communication about you.'

'A communication? From whom?'

'You can't guess? Do you think you can drop from his sight so easily, above all in Malomba?'

'The *Teacher*,' she said. 'What a fool I am. Of *course*. Oh, isn't that just like the Master, Zo? He knows everything, thinks of everything.' Abruptly, feeling they were so cared for although so far from home brought a rush of tears to her eyes. 'Oh, divine. It just flows and flows. There's no end to it, is there?'

'Probably not,' said Ong Mokpin. 'At any rate he told me to expect you, described you and your lovely daughter and said you were staying at the Golden Fortune Hotel. I myself left a message for you there.'

'Oh dear,' said Tessa. 'I'm afraid we're at the Nirvana. The Golden Fortune has been burnt down.'

'You surely are misinformed, Mrs Hemony?' Only hours ago Mr Mokpin had been lying on a vinyl couch on the top floor of the Golden Fortune, being assisted in his recovery from a sauna by two ten-year-old Chinese girls with tiny, fluttery hands.

'I thought Lucky said . . . ?' She looked for confirmation at Zoe. 'I suppose he made a mistake. Anyway, bliss. It doesn't matter. Here we are, as you can see. Not striving, not grasping, but itching to know what you've got in all these bottles.'

'To business then.'

It seemed to Zoe they spent hours in that stuffy room while her mother gave little cries and made lists. Certainly Ong Mokpin appeared learned. Latin phrases mingled with strange native names as stopper after stopper was eased and the essence assayed. After a time she became drowsy with the heat and fumes and voices and longed to be somewhere sharper and higher. She half-dreamed of the days she had spent with Ed in the thin air of Valcognano, talking of not wholly dissimilar things but among the sloping terraces of the Apuan Alps while he paid her court. Why did she think of that now? It came to her suddenly that there was something about this podgy oriental which reminded her of Ed. It was maybe the mixture of languor and beadiness, of a man with each of his feet in a different world who had constantly to shift his weight from one to the other and ended up hovering in a slightly sinister way.

'*Vis medicatrix Naturae,*' Mr Mokpin was saying to her mother. 'And we know how powerful it is, don't we? Now take this, for example. *Melilotus mortionis officinalis* is its name, from the great herbalist who discovered it, Balbus Mortion. A very old man now, of course. Smell. An entirely new clover he found in this country growing only in Saramu Province. A most powerful emmenagogue, better even than fennel and rosemary. I see a big, big market for this. I'm also wondering whether you should get in touch with Mortion himself about a range of Turkish essences? He lives in Istanbul and although he is retired now . . . Yes, you should write him down. His first name is Balbus. Now, as to export and regular orders, I can undertake to supply . . .'

Half an hour later he was saying, 'I truly believe we have several products here which are quite unknown in the West and which could become prodigious sellers. But if I had to choose one it would be this, Mrs Hemony. *Karesh* oil.' The pudding-like fez nodded several times. 'Of course we all know about the powers of auto-suggestion. But *Karesh* oil is truly a potent aphrodisiac for certain people.' A peculiar scent drifted into the room.

'Oh,' Tessa cried, 'I've smelt that before. Here in Malomba. Very recently.'

'Perfectly possible. *Karesh* is a common vine here. It grows everywhere. The flowers smell like this, except of course the oil is immensely concentrated. Actually it takes one hundred and ninety pounds of flowers to make a single ounce.'

Zoe also thought she recognised the smell. Was it back at the hotel? Instead of Ed she found herself thinking of Lucky, since smells had that strange power of abruptly banishing an image and replacing it with something quite else. He had a nice aura. As bell-boys went he was really rather a handsome little brat. Well, perhaps not *that* little; more or less her own age, although his voice wasn't very low yet. He undoubtedly had lovely long eyelashes.

'Packaging . . . Shipping . . . Pure Light Products . . .'

At last it was over and Zoe gently woke their guide who was slumped on his sack. Mr Bundash gave a squeak and brushed waking tears from his eyes. 'Oh dear. Terrifying dreams, young madam,' he murmured.

It was now long past midday and by the time he had led them back out of the labyrinth of the Wednesday Market Tessa and Zoe thought he looked so weary they insisted he should have lunch with them. Out of deference they ate in a Moslem restaurant. Plates of fluffy rice and delicately spiced pulses restored them although the food, coming on top of the morning's heat and scents, made Zoe still drowsier. She thought of Lucky again and wondered what girls of her own age did in Malomba. Suddenly she felt the urge to get away from her mother for a bit, to be a little wild. As they left the restaurant she was full of sleepy yearnings for mild rebellion, and had slouched maybe half a mile beneath the blows of the sun before she was aware they had stopped and that her attention had been caught.

'The place,' Mr Bundash was saying, 'has a thoroughly evil reputation, I regret to tell you.' He was indicating something called the Punk Panther, which was possibly a bar or a restaurant or a night club or all three. It was painted black, including the window panes. It appeared quite shut at the moment and not a sound came from within. A black cat dozed on its threshold as if equably waiting; it wore a tiny brass ring in one ear. 'They opened it about three years ago to take commercial advantage of the sudden increase in tourism. It quickly became known far and wide as a focus for immorality and drug-taking. A certain misguided tourist handbook – it only takes one! – saw fit to mention that there are particular substances, plants and so on, growing in the forests hereabouts which have unfortunate hallucinogenic properties. Among these, I am informed, are certain of the species *amanita* and *psilocybe*. Being a local product they are of course exceedingly cheap.

'You may imagine the rest for yourselves, madams. By word of mouth the notoriety of this establishment quickly spread, inevitably attracting what one is forced to call "the hippy element" as distinct from the spiritual seekers to which Malomba has long been accustomed and which it still welcomes with open arms. Woe to this city!' cried Mr Bundash mournfully, as might any official guide on seeing his home town degenerate. At the same time he kept a covert eye on Zoe since he was paid a commission by The Punk Panther's management for any custom he might steer their way. She struck him as evincing a curiosity whose offhandedness was surely the result of her mother's standing right beside her. 'All-night dancing,' he added gloomily. 'Loud music. Cheap hamburgers.' He shook his head.

When mother and daughter finally reached the hotel they retired at once to darkened rooms.

❧⚜☙

Laki was crossing the Nirvana's back-yard in the remains of twilight. His tuneless whistle told of a pleasant sundownish feeling of having spent the day well. It was largely drowned by the clarions, drums, gongs and wails with which the city's religious greeted the night. As he walked he bounced an empty plastic gallon container on alternate knees. Being off duty, he had changed out of his white cotton uniform and was wearing dark shorts and T-shirt better suited to stealth and minor villainy. Over one shoulder was slung a small bag.

He bonged the container off the goat's rump as he passed it and faded among the tattered banana plants. These leaned their juicy boles drunkenly on the fringes of the tiny patch of land which Mr Muffy had not yet sold to the Bank of the Divine Lotus. Beyond them lay a fence of vertical stakes marking the beginning of the Redemptorist Fathers' garden.

Reaching this Laki pulled out a loose stake, stood it aside and squeezed through the gap. The territory on the other side felt immediately different, not merely because it was forbidden but because it was so lush. At once he was in near-jungle, a forty-yard belt of which separated him from the nearest tongue of deer-cropped grass. He and Raju had once taken pains to approach the toddy palms by varied routes, but their daily undetected journeys had made them careless and between them they had worn a distinct trail. Arriving at the right tree, Laki took from the bag his curved knife which he stuck through his belt, as well as a short length of stout rope. He tied the container to his belt by its handle, stepped out of his rubber slippers, flung the rope around the trunk and began to climb with a hopping motion, knees sticking out at froglike angles on either side.

This method of climbing a palm was hard work and the rope wound about his hands hurt. Had this been a legitimate enterprise he would long ago have hacked hand- and foot-holds into the fibrous wood, but even Raju – whose age was against him for climbing trees after a night's sitting behind the hotel desk – had vetoed this in favour of discretion. As a matter of fact it was a source of pride and pleasure to them both that they should be able to practise their country-boy skills inside the city boundaries.

He reached the top of the palm with early moonlight glinting dully on the knifeblade and swung himself up into thick fronds, panting slightly and squatting down to rest. Between his feet jutted the decapitated stalk of the tree's flower, its bleeding end enclosed by a bamboo cylinder. He unhitched this and, finding a fragment of mosquito netting stashed in a cleft, strained the contents of the bamboo into his plastic container. There seemed to be about a quart of the liquid, an excellent haul. He cut a sliver off the end of the stalk as precisely as a chef slicing cucumber, for the stump tended to heal itself during the day. Having replaced the bamboo, he pushed the knife back in his belt and returned to earth. The entire operation had taken four minutes and in that time true night had fallen. He shouldered his bag and retraced his steps for ten yards but then struck off at a tangent, emerging beneath the cloud-tree.

Nearly opposite, across a strip of grass and amid a whirl of fireflies, stood the Fathers' ornamental pagoda. In front lay the hump of the miniature stone bridge and a black meander of streamlet. The pagoda glimmered white against the vegetation like a chess piece. Laki had little doubt he was unobserved. At this time, he knew, the Fathers would be sitting down to dinner in their bungalow, sparks of whose lights could occasionally be glimpsed seventy yards off through the leaves. Nonetheless, it was not unknown for one of them to go for a stroll, so rather than walk boldly across the lawn he chose to sidle along the edge of the trees to the bridge and flit across it. Now if he stood with his back to the pagoda, his view was of the upper stories of the Hotel Nirvana as they rose above the foliage. Since so few of its rooms were presently occupied it was mainly a dark bulk with here or there a yellow light. One of these might have marked Mrs Hemony's room but the beautiful Zoe's, overlooking the roof of the BDL next door, remained invisible. He sighed but took heart from his own rooftop domain, clearly outlined against an opalescent drift of the Milky Way.

Dropping his bag, Laki carefully approached the pagoda's doorway. Occasionally Father McGoohan would spend a reflective hour sitting inside, for a stone bench lined each of the little room's six walls. Tonight there was no one, merely some dark clots on the floor which he knew to be monkey-dirt. Returning to his bundle, he took out a coil of washing-line appropriated from the Nirvana and tied one end to the bag, the other to his belt. Then he shinnied up the wall to the pagoda's first storey, using the easy handholds offered by its scrolls of exuberant decoration, and squeezed in through a narrow window slit. Inside was a smaller version of the room downstairs but without the benches.

His discovery of this chamber, which was just wide enough to lie down in but in which he had to crouch, had actually been made from his own eyrie. With a pair of binoculars borrowed from a tourist's room, he had deduced that the pagoda must consist of a series of ever-smaller chambers rather than being hollow throughout. He knew this because the monkeys had made the same discovery and could sometimes be seen gallivanting in its cells and grimacing from its windows. They even swarmed up the flanged pinnacle on top and from there swung into the trees whose branches dipped conveniently close.

Laki had long since investigated the structure from top to bottom, but had found only the first floor habitable. The diminishing size of the upper chambers made them suitable only for monkeys. They were full of mud-brick chips from his own rooftop target practice, as well as any amount of twigs and excrement. He had decided to keep this first storey monkey-free by setting traps. He caught several quite painfully and they had been variously boiled, roast, curried and stewed. After a while the monkeys became more prudent and although they could still now and then be seen using the pagoda as a climbing frame and cavorting in its ground-floor room, they rarely went into his chamber. Every so often a new generation was born and he had to set his traps again, but it was comparatively easy to discourage them.

On the other hand they still stole any small object he left

in the room, so it was bare but for the motheaten carpet he had installed (until lately the one article of luxury in Room 41) and a wooden box too heavy for the monkeys to lift. This had originally been made to hold the hotel's fuses and wiring, but before it could be put up Laki had spotted that it would just fit through one of the pagoda's narrow embrasures. It was wide and flat and weighted with catapult ammunition. Besides these pebbles it contained a box of matches and a stump of candle, as well as various snares and nooses made of stainless steel wire.

Now he hauled up his bag after him and added to the box several purloined mosquito coils with their flimsy metal stands. Then he sat in the darkness with the crown of his head touching the cement ceiling. He was excited by this room in some way – excited by *concealment*, by knowing of secret niches where he could sit or lie unsuspected. He took delight in coming and going between mysterious haunts known to himself all over Malomba. The creek in the river where he and Jason had swum that morning was merely one of several places he visited regularly, setting traps and picking fruit or simply lying in a shady nook away from the dust and traffic.

Here in the pagoda was a den where he could be the tiger in the garden with his glossy eyes and pelt, full of power. It was a certainty of his that one day when he was a man and married with a family he would still have such places to pass private hours – not doing anything particularly, but just being able to rejoice in a necessary latency. He liked this chamber's smallness. He liked the fact that it reminded him of his room on the roof – even that here, too, a vine had twined itself about the pagoda and hung a spray of flowers and gourds in through two of the six window slits. Periodically the Fathers' gardener hacked it back, but the ubiquitous vine was never daunted for long.

He sat for a while in the dark taking swigs of warm toddy. The vespertine ceremonials were over; even the pro-

100

cathedral's mournful Lenten tolling had ceased. Instead, the comparative silence of natural sounds filled the night. Frogs roared from the edge of the stream down below, a mosquito whined about his eyelids. Putting an ear to the plastic container, he listened to the soft fizz of toddy fermenting. He mustn't drink too much, he thought, otherwise he would wind up like Raju; the porter would anyway complain that there wasn't enough to see him through his night's vigil. What was more, he had not yet had supper and at this very instant Raju might be polishing off his portion as well. He climbed down to the ground, put the rope back in his bag and set off for the fence. Toddy made his step light and he was whistling again as he reached the gap and wormed through.

A hand fastened on his T-shirt and pulled.

'Little pus-bubble. Oh yes, now we have you,' said Mr Muffy's voice in accents of real satisfaction, and Laki found himself dragged through the hole even before he had time to jettison the toddy. 'And what have *you* been doing, swine-face? What evil adventure is it this time?' He jerked the container from his bell-boy's grasp and shook it at eye-level. 'Kerosene, is it? A bit of fire-raising, maybe, to chase away boredom? But no,' he said, affecting to avert his face fastidiously, 'our breath gives us away. Pure essence of carrion, boy. You've a stench on you like a toddy-shop harlot.'

It was most unfortunate that Mr Muffy had been in the yard, for normally he went home a good two hours earlier. Today, however, the proprietor had become absorbed by the new adding machine whose buttons he had now mastered. He was about to embark on a great Plan to take the Nirvana up-market in a single dazzling move, to engage the Chinese on their own ground. The idea had come to him all at once, as such things did to men of vision. The monopoly the Chinese enjoyed enabled them to fix their prices scandalously high. If he couldn't provide the same standards for a third of the price and still turn a decent profit, then he didn't deserve to be a porter in the Wednesday Market. The prospect inflamed and exhilarated him. In sober moments, however, he knew he was going to need allies. Apart from the Chinese themselves, there were powerful cabals in town who would have to be sweetened.

Part of the solution, he knew, lay with the plain-clothes police. They demanded regular payment and occasional tidbits, but it was worth it in return for being thought a good citizen. If he was hoping to compete with hotels such as the Golden Fortune and the Seven Blessings, he would need at the very least to provide a massage service. He had once heard Mr Botiphar, the Mayor's brother, say that foreigners also liked video films of dwarves giving each other colonic irrigations, and suddenly he had felt completely out of his depth. If that was what it took to stay on top in the hotel business, then so be it; but it was evident that the advice and cooperation of the police would be essential. He had hitherto kept his dealings with them to a nervous minimum but could sense that this would no longer suffice. They liked active compliance, they liked to be kept informed. He sighed. The world of big business was indeed hard. One needed enterprise, sure enough; but one also had to become involved in all sorts of distasteful politicking and grovelling . . . Still, he thought, he was equal to the challenge.

Mr Muffy had fed some projected figures into his machine and the little scroll of paper it spat out caused him much satisfaction. Locking up his office, he was just setting off to tell his wife that if she behaved herself he might soon buy her the gold lamé Hindu pantaloons she coveted when he remembered she had asked him to take a look at the goat and see if it was fat enough to be eaten. He was prodding it when Laki's familiar whistle from beyond the bananas had caught his ear. Now the sight of his bell-boy standing there in shorts and reeking of drink made all too clear the Nirvana's need for radical change.

'Knife,' he said contentedly, having seized the bag and shaken out its contents. 'Rope. Looks to me like a clear case of breaking and entering premises at present unknown. But we'll find out, won't we? Or – no, I've got it. We were bringing our dying mother a life-saving draught of her favourite drink, weren't we? We had to penetrate the isolation ward of Malomba General Hospital. The knife was in case you met with opposition from the nursing staff. Of course. Well, I'm deeply touched, boy; deeply touched . . .' And more in the same ironic vein, during which his grip shifted from the bell-boy's T-shirt to his ear.

Laki, waiting with apparent submission, debated whether to punch his employer in the kidneys and have done with it. In addition to being wonderfully satisfying, it would bring to an end all vacillation and ensure his having to move on. But it would also throw away unfinished all the work he had been putting into the Hemonys. Besides losing his room, he would be banished for ever from the sight of Zoe. Despite the pain in his ear (for Mr Muffy was all the while leading him off through the yard, the kitchens, and along the passage to his office behind the front desk) Laki decided to endure. An end to his troubles was in sight and it would be a pity to spoil it all . . . He would not have been able to say quite how his troubles were going to end, only that he had a definite feeling about the foreign family with which he was building up such cordial relations. Kindness did not go unrewarded, he knew, especially when one was dealing with spiritual visitors. And anyway, foreigners of all kinds were notorious for their impulsive acts of generosity to evade embarrassment, as well as for their miraculous power to change people's lives.

'. . . and then I think we'll telephone the Beetles and give their canes some practice. Warm up that juicy little rump of yours, turdlet, h'm? Oh turdlet, turdlet. It's a criminal child I've been feeding and housing all these years. Dear, dear . . .'

They rounded the corner and there were the Hemonys at the unattended front desk. At once Mr Muffy's hand left Laki's ear-lobe and went around his shoulder as he switched to English.

'Good evening, ladies,' he greeted them jovially. He gave Laki the simulacrum of an affectionate pat on the shoulder. 'Poor boy,' he explained vaguely, as if to dismiss him.

'We want to thank you for lending him to us this morning,' said Tessa. 'Jason had a wonderful time, didn't you, Jay? and we're really grateful. Children don't always want to drag around after adults, do they? Especially boys. They're so bouncy and independent.'

Mr Muffy was smiling bleakly, hand apparently frozen to Laki's shoulder.

'I'm sure you found you could spare him after all, didn't you?' Tessa went on. The proprietor was not certain whether she had seen him pulling the little maggot along by the ear but her next remark made him think she had. 'Young people need their time off, Mr Muffy, especially when they're far from home and worried about their mothers being ill.' This made her glorious daughter shoot her a glance he couldn't begin to interpret. 'Compassion is all, isn't it? To be harsh and lacking in sympathy is only another form of *grasping*, you know. We certainly hope to be seeing a lot more of our young friend while we're staying here in your excellent hotel.'

This sally, not least the protective phrase 'our young friend', faced Muffy with the inevitable. He gave the bell-boy a final pat, his one concession to his feelings being to maintain the smile while lapsing out of English long enough to remark, 'What a lucky turdlet it is to have this silly foreign cow on his side. But she'll be leaving soon *and then what fun there'll be.*'

Laki favoured him with a confident grin and with dazzling impertinence unhitched his bag from his employer's fingers. 'Good night, sir,' he said in English. 'Good night, missus. Good night, miss.' He winked at Jason and walked jauntily off towards the back regions. On the way he met Raju coming from the kitchen wiping his mouth with the back of his hand and belching cardamom fumes. 'I've been caught, uncle,' he explained softly in the passageway. 'I'm afraid there's no toddy tonight. Muffy's at the desk and he's furious.'

'Oh dear, I am a bit late, it's true,' admitted Raju. 'There was such a lot to eat tonight. I'd better go at once.'

Laki watched him go, frowning at the old man's servile haste before turning back towards the kitchen to see if there was anything left. What scraps he could find he took straight up to his room, recognising the need to make himself scarce for the rest of the evening. Sitting beneath the pergola of vines chewing an end of sausage with a lump of stale *laran* bread, he reviewed recent events. Unfortunate, no doubt about that; but nothing like as disastrous as they would have been before the advent of the Hemonys. He thought of the two hundred *piku* the missus had so promptly given him and felt a half-erotic, half-sentimental swelling at her kindness and the circumstances which had provoked it.

He had passed the day in a cocoon of amazement at how easy it was after all to get on in this world. One simply wept a little at the right moment and in the right company. There had been more to it than that, he knew, but he was vaguer about the other magic component and settled for repeating to himself his insight that these were people who wanted something to happen. And maybe old Raju had been right, too: *Never steal a watch when you can steal a heart*. He spat an intractable lump of gristle over the edge of the roof and then couldn't resist looking to see if it had hit anything interesting in the street below.

Even if something went badly wrong with these people – Laki resumed his seat and his chewing – there were all the other foreigners in town. Having refined one's technique, whatever it was, it could presumably be applied to anybody.

Suddenly he saw himself as a pioneer. He would no longer be a bell-boy or a washer-up, another of Malomba's shiftless band of skivvies and menials who barely managed to support themselves, let alone anybody else. No more would he send home irregular remittances to keep his family an inch above disaster. Instead he would be earning the sort of money to change their status once and for all. Architect of the family's fortune, he would himself buy the twelve-horsepower petrol engine which would transform his father's fishing. (He saw the hired jeep bouncing among the palms towards their house, the crated engine gleaming in the back; he saw his family's surprise at this unexpected vehicle as they ran up in the dust cloud of its halting; he saw his father's tears when he finally realised the motor was for him.)

All this Laki clearly saw, and much besides. He saw his mother with new pots and pans and her own private medicine cabinet of antibiotics. He saw his sisters in new dresses, his brothers with air rifles instead of catapults. He saw the plot of land behind their hut expanding and swallowing up the neighbours', stocked with ever-increasing herds of goats and pigs . . . What nothings were the Muffys of the world! Acidulous men in their fifties with their crummy businesses, just keeping afloat by dint of wearisome fiddles and sharp practice. That was no way forward for a boy – a young man, rather – with ambition and real earning potential. One day he would eat Mr Muffy alive. He would come back and simply buy him out. Then, scorning all attempts by the BDL next door to do a deal, he would tear down the Nirvana and . . . and . . . of course, put up the Auld Strait Kirk of Laki, Malomban Rite. Then he would really start making money as part of the city's religious establishment.

And punctually his mind skidded round to the tableful of virgins and his eyes lifted to the glowing ruby light of the Lingasumin, whence came so much imaginative strength.

He shifted his seat. It was an erotic business, glimpsing the future. The mere planning of it, the anticipation of power and the freedom to act was enough to make his fingertips unconsciously brush upwards at the corners of his mouth, to stray across his upper lip, chin and throat as he stared out across the holy city towards a morrow of his own creating.

Tonight the future collapsed before two obtrusive chunks of the present: this fresh trouble with Mr Muffy and his mother's illness. 'Flu was one thing, but he was superstitious about having wished scarlet fever on her for momentary effect. It might come true. He was glad he had tracked down the dried-fish merchant who was an old and trusted messenger for both Raju and himself, coming and going regularly between the east coast and Malomba. But the man had not been due to return to Saramu until this evening – might only just this minute be leaving – so the money wouldn't reach her until late tomorrow or even the day after. Not perfect, but it couldn't be helped.

Less perfect still was Mr Muffy's threat to call in the Beetles. These were the holy city's plain-clothes police, so named because in addition to black slacks they wore reflecting sunglasses for sinister effect, even at night. The Beetles had their own system of justice and were the lawless law; one did anything to avoid falling into their hands. They controlled most of the rackets in town while deciding for themselves who or what was undesirable. Of late they had prospered mightily from the tourist boom, especially from the appetite for *sima* displayed by what Tominy Bundash had described as 'the hippy element'. But there appeared to be an imponderable line drawn between the encouragement of this trade and its suppression. Quite often the flogged bodies of pushers or ordinary vagrants were found on rubbish-dumps in Malomba's untouristed outskirts, reminders that the Beetles never shot or strangled or knifed but always caned their victims to death. Among the poor it was commonly held that anybody might be eligible for 'tenderising'; enough that a squad of Beetles in one of their scarlet jeeps be bored or drunk and pick a quarrel with someone who answered back. They seldom interfered with foreigners, content merely to stare from a passing vehicle at anyone they thought sufficiently scruffily-dressed to be unwelcome on account of poverty. Insofar as the Beetles were ever pleased to see anyone, they were happiest with a rich, conventionally dressed foreigner who put up at a good Chinese hotel and sent out for quantities of *sima* and little massage-girls at night, while tottering out for some psychic surgery by day.

Laki, as he himself well knew, fell precisely into the category of the Beetles' preferred victim. He had no illusions about what would happen if Mr Muffy did send for them, but it was obviously just another of the man's empty threats, for what would he stand to gain? In the event Laki might not merit tenderising the first time, but he would certainly be meted out some exemplary treatment as a warning. Anyway, once you had claimed their attention you became trouble by association and no one in town would ever give you another job.

He shuddered a little, but phlegmatically. If the worst came to the worst, he always had his catapult and it was well known that the one thing the Beetles couldn't do was *run*. Free drinks and meals from prudent hoteliers and restaurateurs, to say nothing of driving endlessly about in jeeps, had rendered them quite unfit for running. 'They should run on their hands,' went the stock Malomban joke. 'God knows their arms get enough exercise.'

Tonight when Laki finally went into his hutch to sleep, he locked the door with especial care although more from caution than real anxiety. The Beetles were just something one lived with. Meanwhile, a morning's swimming with Jason in the water hole as well as his exertions in the Redemptorist Fathers' garden had left him with a pleasant weariness and he soon fell asleep on his straw mat.

An unknown time later he sat up abruptly on the floor, trying to remember what had woken him. Then the noise came again. Someone had opened the hatchway on to the roof and then closed it. At this very moment, maybe, fat men in slacks and sunglasses were surrounding the dovecote, canes tapping softly and expectantly against their legs.

❦

When Tessa had said good night to the children and gone to her room, she found that despite the day's wanderings through the Wednesday Market and the excitement of discovering all the unfamiliar essences in Mr Mokpin's shop, she was not yet ready for sleep. She went to the window and leaned out, savouring the night air. The moon which had earlier lit Laki's climb of the pagoda was now nearing its zenith and striking blue metallic gleams off blades of vegetation in the garden below. A thick whirr of frogs and lizards and crickets rose up as from a generator. Fancifully, she thought it was this machine which kept the night ticking over, the sheened leaves stirring, the moon pouring out its light and the fireflies aloft. Facing away from the city's neon prodigality, she could almost believe herself miles from the nearest town and the mouldy hothouse fragrance that of virgin jungle.

On arriving, she remembered, she had thought Malomba was going to be playful and numinous. Nothing had yet happened to change that view, although the peculiar mix of these elements was not quite what she had expected. Her few days here had indeed been numinous to the point of overdose. Never before had she visited so many holy places, each with its own distinctive approach to the Other. This was unmistakably a place of the spirit, one in which people had always taken spiritual things seriously and lived their

109

lives accordingly. And yet she could not deny that the vibrations were a little weaker, perhaps, a little more elusive than she might have predicted.

Undoubtedly, too, she had encountered much that was playful. Their guide, Mr Bundash: was he not sweet with his theological nightmares and pompous rote-learning? His dismay at being overheard and corrected by the Spodist High Priest was particularly touching; for a moment the timid, bewildered-child look on his face had made her want to take him in her arms and comfort him. That would never have done, she smiled at the cloud-tree's glimmering outline. As for the boy, Lucky, he was playfulness incarnate. But underneath his coltish comings and goings, could she not glimpse elements of disquiet? She had clearly seen Mr Muffy tugging the child along by the ear with a look of venom which bespoke imminent punishment, whether merited or not. What trivial crime had he committed? Or was he simply the virtual slave of a cruel and sadistic employer? What was going on below?

That was it, thought Tessa, as she let her eyes drift out of focus so her retinas bacame mere blackboards for the fireflies' scribbles. Behind this lush and exotic town were constant intimations of menace. Vertiginous pits kept opening up beneath the most innocent things. A scarlet jeep passing in the street; fish dying in the market; a fruit with deadly seeds. Even a ride on a children's train led to bloodshed. And behind Lucky's tearful story about his mother's illness what narratives of peasant misery, of hardship and separation might not be read?

Leaving the window for a moment, she fetched from the bedside the Master's greatest work, *The Fragrant Mirror*. This book contained his distilled wisdom and countless million copies of it in one hundred and thirty-eight different languages were abroad in the world. These were mostly cheerful paperbacks whose covers depicted Swami Bopi Gul himself seated in a meadow deep with flowers and holding up a mirror in which was reflected a single lotus bloom. Her own copy, though, was one of a special autographed edition limited to favoured disciples, and had black leather binding embossed with a yellow mandala. Opening it she turned to a chapter entitled 'The Mirror Speaks' and re-read the following, heavily underlined, passage:

17. O my friend, would you expect a pine tree to sprout from an egg? Then do not expect from me what is not in my nature to be. Hold me up to evil and you will see it reflected unwaveringly in my heart. Hold me up to good and you will see that, too, no less clearly. I am a mirror, so I may not strive to change what I see. I am a mirror, so I may not grasp at one image instead of another. All I can do is reflect truthfully everything passing before me.

18. You say, 'How inert, how useless! Is that all you can do for a world so muddied and unhappy?'

19. And I reply, 'Yes.' But that 'all' is everything, and to do it is the hardest thing there is. For to give in to the temptation to 'right' 'wrongs' is to intervene. And to intervene is always to stir up the mud and make things still muddier, yet unhappier, even though in the short term this may not be apparent.

20. But if by supreme effort I can keep my heart unclouded and crystal clear, then the world will be confronted by true reflections of how it is. Thus 'evil' on seeing me will in time weary of its own face and be dissatisfied, while 'good' will in time weary of its own face and yearn to dissolve.

21. Never doubt this truth, my friend: the world is like your body and likewise contains the power to heal itself. Only do nothing to destroy its mysterious balance. Restrain your egoistical desire to change it according to your own ideas of morality. Like any flower it is too intricate and delicate for your understanding.

22. For what are 'good' and 'evil' but two faces of an imagined cloud?

23. He who yearns to dissolve knows that bliss is where there are no clouds of any kind. Not striving, not grasping, he is in bliss.

He makes himself pure mirror. What, then, is this Meditation of the Mirror? I will tell you. It is this: *What is it that one clear mirror sees when confronted by another? And where is that image formed?* Think on this, my friend.

These familiar words generally brought tears to her eyes. It was one of the Teacher's own preferred passages and whenever she read it she could hear his slow, resonant delivery during which he never looked at the page but always at a spot on the ground about eighteen inches beyond as if at an invisible autocue. It was thus, in a semi-trance, he would quietly declaim whole chapters at a time, a faculty which merely reinforced the fame of the astonishing circumstances in which the book had been written.

Gul had not been a swami then, but just any young man of twenty born in a village a few miles from Bombay who had gone to the city in search of work. He had found employment in a warehouse, but was always on the point of being sacked for his dissolute lifestyle. One day – stupefied with drink and *bhang* – he fell asleep in a huge crate, was nailed up for a prank and transported to the goods yard. There he was loaded into a freight waggon together with seven similar crates containing equipment and stationery for blind schools in Gujarat state. He came round in pitch darkness and from the muffled sounds and motion deduced what had happened. Realising that nobody would hear him if he shouted, he conserved his energy and what little air there was until the train stopped. When it did, he shouted for hours but nobody came.

What Gul could not know was that the train had been uncoupled and his waggon was now standing with a dozen others, padlocked and deserted, in a siding on the outskirts of Bannapur. His legend began with the unloading of the waggon three weeks later. If the navvies were puzzled by the powerful scent of flowers which rolled out as they opened the doors, they were astonished by what they found in a lidless crate. A young man was sitting in deep meditation.

Before him was a Braille typewriter, beside him a stack of blank pages. Then someone noticed that the pages were not, after all, blank. During those eighteen days Gul, without knowing how to type in any language, still less in Braille, had seemingly composed *The Fragrant Mirror* in pitch darkness and without any food or water. From that moment he became a swami. For all those who cried 'humbug!' and 'stunt!' there were others who had not the slightest doubt of his authenticity.

Tessa herself had never questioned his divinity. Over the years she had, she considered, experienced ample evidence of his powers. He was a wonderful healer: there was no lack of witnesses who could testify to that. Why, then, couldn't he heal her backache the way he healed others? He had taken her hand and she experienced a shock as of electricity strong enough to make her snatch it away with a cry.

'We're too close, sister,' the Teacher said. 'You see? Our magnetism is not right. I probably couldn't heal a member of my own family, either.' He gave a deprecatory laugh. 'I can't always heal myself, even. You remember the wound on my foot? It was you who healed that.'

She well remembered the occasion early on in her discipleship. They had been climbing the path up to Valcognano with two mules laden with supplies, the Teacher walking barefoot beside her. It was November and the stone steps were partly hidden beneath drifts of golden leaves through which they rustled. Suddenly he had stopped and brought a foot out into a shaft of sunlight. Stuck at an angle in its sole was a curved piece of iron which she had taken for an old mule shoe, but which she later found was the reinforcement from the heel of a boot. At any rate his foot was impaled by a pair of rusty nails. She had looked helplessly at it with a cry almost of fear, for she had never touched any part of his body, had only ever felt the energy in his hands.

'Why not remove it, sister?' he had asked with a smile. 'If you would be so kind?'

And she had knelt in the leaves and tugged the iron out
and at once two streams of blood came from the punctures.
She would never forget that extraordinary instant: his
smiling down with a kind of mischievous serenity, the spots
of his blood on the leaves which sparkled in the sun's rays
like spinels, the autumnal smell of leaf-mould.

'Now stop the bleeding, sister.'

'I . . . I don't know how, Master.' She looked about her
for recognisable herbs, but could see only brambles.

'Just touch it with your hand and mind.'

And when nervously she had passed her fingertips
beneath his sole, they came away with no trace of blood on
them. She was amazed, but before she could look under his
foot at the wounds themselves he had set it firmly down.

'Go on!' he shouted, pointing towards the mules' retreat-
ing rumps as they plodded upward. 'When in doubt, *go on*!
See – even mules know that!'

They had resumed their journey, but when they arrived
in Valcognano he said, 'You are troubled, my dear Tessa?'

'Forgive me, Teacher. I didn't know a great swami could
tread on a nail. I never thought of you as being . . . well,
vulnerable.'

'It wouldn't surprise me if there were much you didn't
know,' he said. 'For example, you never knew you were a
healer, did you?'

'Oh, I'm not, Teacher. I'm just a student of herbs. I know
a bit about what not to do, that's all. Maybe we should put
something on your wound now in case it infects?'

'If you think it necessary,' he laughed. 'I'm in your hands,
doctor.'

And he had raised his foot so that she could see the sole:
pale, unmarked, without a trace of blood or puncture and
with not even so much as a stain of leaf-mould.

'You were looking at the wrong foot,' Jason told her in one
of his moods when she was recounting this story, not for the
first time. What had upset her was not the crotchety

cynicism of the suggestion, the childish scoffing, but that her son had so unerringly placed in her mind a simple alternative explanation for an incident which held for her nothing but sacred significance. The worst of it was not that it made her doubt, but that she couldn't put it out of her head.

Since then it had been Zoe, strangely enough, who had contributed most to Tessa's disquiet. She had gone to England to spend a fortnight with her father. Bruce now had another family with whom she seemed to get on well, to her mother's concealed regret. Zoe had returned looking thoughtful. One day she said to no one in an exasperated voice, 'So fucking what?' She was standing in the open doorway of their house in Valcognano, staring out across the blue panorama of adjacent mountains. Behind her at the kitchen table Tessa was wrapping bundles of dried comfrey.

'What do you mean, Zo?'

Zoe gave herself a shake, surprised at being caught speaking aloud.

'Just thinking.' There was a long silence. 'But so fucking what, all the same. It's a cultural thing, that's all, isn't it? All this Indian stuff. I don't mean the healing: I suppose that's good and useful in any language. But why are we expected to go along with all the other crap about reincarnation? You don't believe in the Christian version of heaven, why should you believe in cycles of re-birth? You're not an Indian. Anyway, I'm not an Indian and I don't believe a word of it. But the point is, even if it was true I'd still say so fucking what? It's crazy to live your whole life just trying to avoid being born as a woodlouse the next time around. If there *is* a next time; which there won't be.'

This naked barrage had caught Tessa unprepared. She had floundered and continued to do so. Her children were growing up. Old alliances were shaky. An emptiness was in the air.

Now she leaned on the window-sill of her room in the

Nirvana with *The Fragrant Mirror* closed on one thumb. *That* was the unease which Malomba diffused stealthily behind its thick scents and lavish spectacle. Never before had she been in a place so quick to take root in the mind. A difficult, significant place where she had arrived with last-ditch punctuality: in her forties, not a moment too soon. She might pretend to rejoice in whatever gave a salutary poke to one's spiritual complacency, but she had not bargained for Malomba's hidden glands. The holy city itself was an organism, an edifice of rich and eclectic design. It was an imaginative, aspiring structure; but one around the galleries of whose dome an insidious whisper clearly carried: *So fucking what?* Oh, poison incense . . . The only certainty was backache. And with it something as banal as being lonely.

Suddenly she became aware of what she was doing. She was leaning on a sill which ought not to have been there. Examining, she found that it had been replaced inexpertly but sturdily at a slight angle. She smiled, imagining Lucky at work with a borrowed hammer. Or stolen? She had the urge to find out whether it was really he who had mended the window, whether she had thanked him enough for giving Jason such a lovely time, why that villainous-looking hotel proprietor seemed to have it in for him. She glanced at her clock. Only just past eleven. In any case, she was wide awake and really did want to look at Malomba from the roof. Honestly, really did.

From Jason's enthusiastic description of visiting the bell-boy's den, Tessa had a fair idea of how to reach the roof. She went through the door at the end of the corridor which led on to the servants' stairwell, holding it open long enough to memorise by the spill of yellow light how the last flight turned, then went through into the darkness and closed it behind her. She climbed the steps, hand out-stretched, and came at last to the hatchway. Pushing at yielding wood, she climbed through. Against the town's neon spangles stood the dark bulk of the dovecote, the vine which largely smothered it giving it the outline of a great heap of briars amid which a white door gleamed. As she crossed to it the scent of vine flowers came to her, together with the memory of Ong Mokpin saying '*karesh*'. Softly she knocked.

There was silence, then a voice, childishly high with nervousness: '*Minu di?*'

'It's me, Lucky. Mrs Hemony. You know, the missus.' She felt an idiot. Why was she here? What was she doing? The door opened a crack.

'Missus? You have trouble?' His sleepy mind was still fixed in its groove of impending threat.

'Oh, Lucky. I'm so sorry. No, no trouble. I'm disturbing you for nothing. I . . . I couldn't sleep and wanted some fresh air so I thought of the roof. Then I remembered Jason telling me you lived up here.'

'Missus, you no disturb. Wait please.' There were soft noises in the darkness ahead; a match flared and revealed the boy crouching on the floor, yawning and lighting a rag stuffed into the neck of a bottle half full of oil. He was naked but for a pair of white undershorts. The orange light which took hold glowed on coppery skin and shone in black eyes raised towards her.

'Lucky! What a lovely room!' She stood just inside the door of the cell admiring its wall of leaves. From behind it came the rustlings and mutterings of pigeons disturbed by voices and light. The boy was now standing awkwardly, slightly trapped. 'Don't worry, I shan't come in.'

'I show outside where can sit. More cooler there. Very beautiful view, missus.'

He moved towards her, so she had no option but to retreat. The smell of the vine in the room was overpowering. She thought she must be at the very centre of the true Malomba, so much did this chamber encapsulate the city she had hoped to find. The religious glow of burning oil, the

117

sumptuous simplicity of the mat on the floor, the indoor tree dripping its incense. The perfume went into her lungs, made her heart pound, her knees unaccountably weak. She backed away from the outline of his bare stomach. He led the way around the hutch to where the vine threw its pergola over the edge of the hotel roof. Only now did she connect her first sight of the Nirvana as a scruffy building with a bush on top with this bowered eyrie overlooking a numinous city.

Tessa allowed herself to be shepherded beneath the leafy canopy and invited to sit on a decayed rattan settee with her feet on the parapet. The bell-boy sat by her ankles with his back to the neon fairyland and gazed up at her face as if trying to puzzle out her heart.

'You like view?' he asked presently. His eyes never left hers.

'Stupendous. You have the most romantic house.' Half a mile away the Glass Minaret stood knee-deep in the profane hues of Chinatown, its lower facets stained with freakish wattages. The Virgin on the pro-cathedral gave Tessa a knowing wink. For a moment she sat awkwardly, unable to think of anything to say. What had she got herself into now? It was too silly. The night air stirred enough to carry a fresh drench of perfume. She reached up and touched a gourd. *'Karesh.'*

'Oh missus, where you hear that? You to learn speaking our language, I think.' The boy looked pleased. 'This National Plant.'

'I never knew there was such a thing . . . The smell's amazing. I've been making arrangements with a man in the Wednesday Market to buy some *karesh* oil to take back with us.'

'How much the price from Mr Mokpin?'

There it was again, she thought: that sense of everybody here knowing better than yourself what you were up to. 'I can't remember.' She added airily, 'Of course I may decide not to buy from Divine Essence at all,' aware how hollow this piece of spurious canniness sounded. 'At any rate I'm not leaving without *karesh* oil.'

'For what you using that, missus?' the boy asked guilelessly.

'Oh, you know, for my work. I need to have as many oils and essences as I can get. I've never come across *karesh* before. It's such a strange smell I want to discover what its properties are . . . Do you understand "properties"? You know, its effects. What it does.'

The boy was looking at her intently. 'We have song here about *karesh*, missus.'

'Sing it for me, go on.'

With no trace of self-consciousness he raised a soft, husky alto in a little tune. To her ignorant ears the words she heard were as follows:

> *Naswal karesh,*
> *sus lil-han;*
> *Gantal karesh,*
> *ān lil-hun.*

'How beautiful,' she said when he had finished. 'That's lovely, Lucky. But what does it mean?'

The translation took some time, fraught as it was with problems of syntax and grammar. Eventually, though, they reached a satisfactory rendering in English:

> Vine in bloom,
> boyish dreams;
> Vine in fruit,
> men are born.

'But,' she objected, 'it doesn't seem to make sense that way. I mean, you'd expect one thing to happen and *then* the other. Look here, though,' she brushed her hand through the leaves above. 'It flowers and fruits at the same time.'

'Oh yes, my missus.'

119

Again that look from beneath long eyelashes, powerfully evoking the night of his distress. 'Have you heard from your mother yet, Lucky?' she asked.

'Not yet, missus. It very too soon. But I giving your kind money to special friend who will taking to my mother. For sure she has antibiotic now.'

'I know here that she's already better.' Tessa tapped the left side of her chest with a serious expression. 'Tell me about your parents, then.'

So he told her, giving much the same account as to Jason, only maybe stressing the tragedy of his exile a little more, rounding out the picture of his family's penniless grind. She found it temporarily subduing, a glimpse of waste on an endless scale; of how for want of trivial sums people were worn away, their children exported, their illnesses uncured. Nothing she didn't know, of course. Had she not visited the slums of Bombay with the Swami? Nor was it something she hadn't made a truce with. Things were as they were. *Acceptance* in its true sense did not mean indifference, after all. It meant: Who could presume to second-guess the infinite cycle of being? or, Who dared judge from this single lifetime the worth of a soul in progress? Come to that, who could assert that Lucky's fisherman father was poised any more perilously on the lip of extinction than was some bloated capitalist back home? Her own father had had a stroke in the lavatory of an American company jet between Galveston and St Louis. He had died at nine o'clock in the morning at twenty-one thousand feet, freshly shaved and breakfasted and not yet turned fifty, on his way to some vital meeting or other. He was found with his trousers down and his head in the washbasin, the agenda for the meeting still clutched in one hand as though in a last attempt to convince the Reaper that his visit was quite unscheduled and there was no way he could be fitted in that morning.

'The whole thing's so inscrutable, isn't it, Master?' she had blurted once in a momentary lapse. 'The whole *thing*.'

120

'So give up scruting,' he had said with his astounding smile. 'Just *be*.'

Tessa now supposed this was her Teacher's version of Zoe's 'So fucking what?' She became aware of pressure against the side of her calf and looking down at the boy found he had allowed his thigh to loll against her. They were a healthily tactile people, she thought, although in the present instance it was presumably the casualness of a child who had not yet learned the language of proximity. Then he slipped a hand over her kneecap and she became even more unsure.

'Oh missus, you so kind to me. So very kind to helping poor bell-boy. Already you good mother to beautiful girl and boy. Already you better mother than my mother because to helping me also.'

'You mustn't say that, Lucky. Your mother loves you very much, I know she does. It's just that because I have a bit more money it's easier for me to *look* like a better mother, perhaps.'

'No no, you better for sure, missus. My mother she sending me here to Malomba when I am little, little boy, maybe eleven years old. You to helping me, even I not your son.' He was embracing her knee now, resting his cheek on it and looking up at her with eyes in whose inky gaze gleamed splinters of reflected neon from Chinatown. He appeared somewhat huddled over his own lap. 'You to helping me, missus.'

'Oh.' She managed a laugh which came out faultily. 'You oughtn't to be sitting down there at my feet, you know. We're equals.' She patted the cane seat beside her. 'Come and sit here.' For she had just remembered that because of the heat she had left off her underwear before dinner, and having an adoring and backlit bell-boy at knee level raised issues of delicacy. He got up, oddly crouched, and sat with much crackling of decrepit wicker. 'That's better. Look, I'm sure I can help you a bit more. I mean, we're not rich or anything and I know we aren't here for very long, but we can certainly do something.'

He met this vagueness by gripping her hand fervently and saying, 'There is something, my missus. But I cannot to asking. No, no.'

'Of course you can, Lucky. You can ask me anything. What is it?' She was already braced for a request for more money.

'I wanting you to . . . No. I . . .' He was shaking his head in the scented night, hair flashing dully in the light of mosques and churches and temples.

'Please, Lucky. We're friends. Anything.'

'I . . . I wanting you to kissing me, missus, like mother. I very lonely boy in this place.'

A vision came to her of this outcast child being led along the corridor by one ear earlier this evening. This evening? It seemed an age ago. Mr Muffy's savage expression rose again in her mind. They had been just in time to protect the poor boy. She slipped an arm comfortingly around his shoulders. Looking down – for his head was indeed lower than hers – she thought to see the glint of tears? sweat? on his face. She bent and gave him a maternal peck on the cheek and tasted salt. The smell of the vine grew stronger; his skin seemed perfumed with it and she wondered whether he actually used *karesh* oil himself. And then she realised that by some mysterious topological shift the cheek beneath her lips had turned into mouth, that she could feel his tongue on hers and could scarcely believe it. At the same time he was gently nudging her spare hand so it, too, settled on altered terrain. She had an absurd flashback image of a grid-patterned tablecloth spread out to dry on the grass behind the house in Valcognano, various tufts and sprigs thrusting it up into damp mountains exactly like those illustrations of geographical relief in school textbooks.

'Oh my missus,' he breathed fragrantly into her mouth. 'You to helping me. Oh so kind. Oh. Yes.'

There was a pause in their speech. Then wicker creaked and a machine in her head came to life and counted One-two-three; four, five. Six. Sev-en. A much longer pause.

'Oh missus.' He rested his head against her bicep and she watched the lights glisten on his chest and stomach as he breathed. 'You to helping me.'

'But is it helping your mother?' she asked facetiously, half-incredulous.

He was also laughing. 'I her boy. You to helping me, you also to helping her.'

'Some boy . . . I think you're like this *karesh* vine, Lucky.'

'You to helping me become man.'

Feeling herself skating foolishly around the edge of a pit of infantilism, Tessa tried for a note of mature practicality. 'Be sure that before we leave I'll give you some money. Promise. Don't worry about anything. We're not the sort of people who break our promises.'

Out in the city various clocks and gongs chimed mid-night. A loudspeaker on the Temple of Ra cleared its throat and intoned a short prayer for the safe passage of the sun in its boat crossing the treacherous waters of Hades. From a far suburb a disturbed rooster added its voice.

'Can I just see your room again?' she asked at length. 'I've honestly never seen a room with a tree in it before.'

This time he took her hand and led her round to the door. Inside, the home-made lamp cast its steady orange glow, adding a sooty perfume to the scent of flowers. An observer at the door would have seen them standing in front of the plant as before an altar, the boy a good head shorter than the woman. At first sight this observer might have thought of a mother and her child, for all that her hair was dusty blonde and his as black as the night sky. But then he might have noticed something not quite expected in the form of their intimacy; have guessed this was no rite but merely a pause in unfinished business. Thus the woman made no move when the boy crossed to the door and shut it. As he did, and just before the crack of light disappeared with the sound of a bolt being shot, his voice could be heard saying softly: 'Now I think I am to loving you, my missus.'

◆◆◆

It was the day of her appointment with *hadlam* Tapranne and Tessa awoke with a pang of apprehension. While she knew there would be no pain, she had nevertheless seen a good many photographs of psychic surgery in progress and they all seemed to show the first inch of a healer's fingers buried in a bloody hole, generally in somebody's abdomen. A further disquieting image was that of a patient with one eye peacefully closed, the other removed from its socket while a Filipino in T-shirt and jeans pulled what looked like a clump of wet hemp from behind it.

Another worry, though, was rather different. She was all too aware that the Master himself had used his influence to get her an appointment with the most famous healer of all; that with considerable trouble she had been fitted into a long list of patients from all over the world, assuredly with ailments far graver than hers. The fact was that after two nights' visits to the hotel roof Tessa's backache had vanished absolutely. She got out of bed without a twinge, could stretch her arms in the shower to meet the brown trickle of water, as limber as she had been at twenty. She dressed, realising the pain had completely left her for the first time in ten years, half moved with gratitude for this unexpected miracle and half panicked that within a couple of hours she could be exposed as a malingerer.

She went to the window. The early sun fell slantingly on the Redemptorist Fathers' garden, sparkling off the last of the dew. Monkeys were dropping like ripe fruit from the trees on to the pagoda's tip, rolling and tumbling down its widening eaves. On the lawn a pair of deer grazed, practically motionless save for a whirring of little tails. Glancing down she could see the splintery, half-moon dents which an unskilful hammer had left around the nailheads in the sill. She gave a fond smile. She had no idea what she was up to, cradle-snatching briefly in this unreal city. Whatever it was, though, she could hardly recall an experience so pungent in its straightforward intensity, so puppyish in its lack of artifice. And the *energy* of the child . . . Tessa smiled again and stretched. She had never imagined there might be something erotic in tuition, still less that it would make her feel young to recall her own learning.

There was a knock on the door. 'Mum?'

Guiltily she turned from the window. She hadn't even dared imagine how awful it would be if the children found out. It was one thing to be bohemian, something else to be a mother. At a pinch Zoe might be induced to understand, but Jason . . . And here he was, more sullen than ever and not meeting her eyes.

'We've decided we're coming with you,' Zoe said.

'Are you quite sure?' Tessa looked more at Jason. 'What about you, Jay? I know it's completely different from watching an operation in hospital and anyway it'll be over in a jiffy, but even so. You might feel a bit queasy, mightn't you? Don't you think it'd be better if—'

'No, I'm coming,' he said, adding quietly, 'I shan't mind if you scream.'

'Oh, Jay. Is that nice?' She laughed brightly. 'What a ghoul you are. Sorry to disappoint you but there'll be no screaming. There won't be any pain at all.'

'How do you know?'

'It doesn't hurt. That's one of the extraordinary things about psychic surgery. You don't imagine all those people would cheerfully submit to pure torture, do you? Film stars and businessmen?'

'Then it's a fake. Of course it's a fake.'

'Fine, Jay, come and see for yourself.'

'I said I was going to, didn't I?'

Had she any lingering idea that it might still be possible to 'borrow' Laki again to entertain Jason in some alternative, boyish pursuit, she was disabused at breakfast. The bell-boy was nowhere in evidence. Nobody bustled up with fresh *laran* loaves or luscious soursops to replace the hotel's regulation fare of cheesy papaya slices. Instead, a young girl with a harelip brought them the usual leathery toast tasting faintly of paraffin. Suddenly Mr Muffy himself came in with a proprietor's empty smile.

'Good morning ladies, gentleman. Is everything to your satisfactions? And what is your itinerary today?'

'This morning we're going to see *hadlam* Tapranne.'

'Ah, the *hadlam*', Mr Muffy said, something approaching respect in his voice. 'Very good man, very famous. You have appointment?'

'Of course,' said Tessa sharply. Then, 'Maybe your bell-boy might show us the way.'

'Alas, no. That is quite impossible. He is not in Malomba.'

Tessa was taken aback by the pang this caused but said, carefully offhand: 'Has he gone to visit his mother, then?'

'He has not. I've sent him to Banji to fetch paint. Can you credit how much it is cheaper to buy to the paint factory than in the shops here in Malomba? Wicked, wicked, the way these Chinese merchants put the prices up. Banji is only six kilometres away and yet a can of paint costing forty-eight *piku* there costs fifty-seven here. Imagine! Are we to believe?' Mr Muffy demanded of his breakfast room, the flabby slices of uneaten toast, the walls spattered with birdshit, 'are we to believe that the transportation of a single can of paint six kilometres costs eight *piku*?'

'Nine,' said Jason.

'Exactly, nine,' agreed Mr Muffy with the impartiality of one for whom figures seldom coincided. 'The Moslems are worse still. The price is the same but when you open the tin it's old, with a skin that thick,' he held finger and thumb half an inch apart, 'and anyway it's never the same colour as on the top. But worst of all are the Hindus. With a great smile they sell you an empty tin. But don't worry,' he said in an unexpected shift, '*hadlam* Tapranne's not like that. No cheating. He's a genuine Malomban like I am. He is our National Healer. I will show you the postage stamp with his picture.'

Ten minutes later the Hemonys caught a motor tricycle flying a yellow pennant which read in English 'Malomba – City of the Gods'. They were taken out to the edge of town, just beyond the park with the miniature railway. There on a quiet avenue running beside the Botanical Gardens a residential quarter with large bungalows was set back in deep plots. It was fronted by practically continuous walls, high and whitewashed, broken by wrought-iron gates and wooden sentry-boxes in which soldiers sat holding ancient rifles across their knees in white-gloved hands.

'Healers' Village,' said the tricycle driver and buzzed off in a cloud of blue smoke.

A succession of guards directed them around several hundred yards of wall and into a humbler entrance in a side road. They soon realised that this was a cantonment of houses rather than a street of individual lots. Directed in at yet another gate, they found themselves in a tyre-worn garden evidently used as a car park. Here several taxis and tricycles stood, drivers squatting beside them playing a game with tossed coins. Nearby was a long-distance coach with smoked windows and a notice on the rear proclaiming its 'AirCon Luxury'. On the sides additional lettering called it 'The Healing Express' with underneath a line of smaller capitals: 'National Spiritist Tours Company'. There was also a minibus which simply bore the name of the Golden Fortune Hotel.

'It's an industry!' exclaimed Zoe.

127

'Proof that it works,' said her mother uneasily. She, too, had misgivings at these signs of package tourism, which were scarcely lessened by notice boards standing beside various paths leading off through the shrubbery towards half-concealed villas. 'Hadlam Mollyko', she read. 'Hadlam Punjee'. Another sign said 'Jesus Bontoc. Original Filipino Healing'.

'Cancer-cancer-cancer,' sang out a little man trotting towards them. 'You have tumour, madam?'

'I *beg* your pardon?'

'*Hadlam* Punjee world's most expertest to psychic lumpectomy, madam. You come. No charge.'

Tessa gave him a look in which she tried to compress her own status: as a healer, as a student of the Way with years of meditation behind her and as someone who lived rough up a mountain. But mostly she tried to radiate serenity at being affiliated to Swami Bopi Gul.

'Womb, madam? *Hadlam* Punjee also very good to womb.'

Behind her she heard Jason giggle. 'I have,' she said, enunciating as clearly as she once had when called upon to read the lesson on Parents' Day, 'an appointment with *hadlam* Tapranne. Tapranne. An appointment. Not Banerjee or whatever his name is. Also, for your unmerited information, my womb is in excellent health.'

The little tout turned, one indifferent hand indicating the rear of the nearest villa, and walked off. Tessa led the way and they came upon a crowd of people clustered around the door of a conservatory.

'*Hadlam* Tapranne?' she asked a face in the crowd.

'Yes, yes, to going inside, madam!'

They were pushed into the conservatory which was full of plants and yet more people waiting. Many of these were obviously ill; several were in wheelchairs, while still others had stained bandages wrapped about them. They seemed to be local people, poorly dressed and gap-toothed, whose

128

sticks and crutches had been cut in the forest. Most contrived to look quite cheerful. One middle-aged man wearing a straw sombrero smiled deferentially on catching sight of Tessa and the children. He half rose and raised his hat enough to reveal two inches of stout iron nail sticking out of the top of his skull before resuming his seat by a clump of cannas.

'Did you see *that*, Zo?' came Jason's awed whisper. His sister pretended to ignore him. '*Madonna cacona.*'

Tessa herded him apart and said in a quiet, fierce voice, 'You are *never* to use that sort of language in a place like this, Jason. *Never*. Is that clear? The right vibrations are critical when someone's healing as you perfectly well know, and that sort of thought is dangerously negative. No, really: I'm not joking, Jay. Sometimes a healer can lose his power in the middle of an operation if there's cynicism around him. Okay?'

At this moment there was a general stir in the room as through a bead-curtained doorway surmounted by a Lions Club plaque filed some large, pale foreigners. Many looked radiant, others were in tears and smiles, a few stared at the ground and shook their heads as they walked. Several had sticks and a couple carried video cameras perched on their shoulders. As they made their way through the waiting patients and out towards the buses, Tessa glimpsed two copies of *The Fragrant Mirror*. She smiled. It was a good omen. All would be well.

Bringing up the rear was a fat man wearing a short-sleeved dentist's smock, puce trousers and a flimsy hay biretta. He stood in the doorway and beamed generally at his departing patients as at those still waiting. Every eye in the conservatory was expectant upon him. His teeth encompassed the Hemonys and passed on. He let fall the heavy strands and disappeared. An Indian lady with a bead in one nostril and a white and gold sari emerged in his stead and spoke to half a dozen of the crowd, including the man in the sombrero. They got up and went through the curtain. She approached Tessa.

'Sister Hemony?' they *pranam*ed 'I'm Sister Savitri. You're so very welcome.' Her smile warmly included Zoe and a rebelliously sulky Jason. 'Our Swami sends his greetings.'

'Oh! You've spoken to him? Is he here in Malomba?'

'No, no. He must be still in America. I think you didn't receive his letter?' From the folds of her sari she produced a familiar, patchouli-scented envelope. It was addressed to Tessa at the Golden Fortune Hotel. 'Because you're at the wrong place you didn't receive it,' this lady said chidingly. 'It arrived yesterday too late to take round to your Nirvana Hotel.'

She opened the letter eagerly. Inside was a sheet of onionskin paper and one unsigned sentence: 'Dearest Tessa – We are with you.' Her eyes filled. 'He thinks of everything. He never lets you go, does he?' The Indian lady smiled on. 'He knows everything.'

'He didn't know where we were staying,' pointed out Jason from behind.

'Come,' said Sister Savitri. 'The *hadlam* is waiting.'

'Oh golly. Now?' She and the children were marshalled through the beaded doorway, down a short passage and into a room rigged as either a church or a theatre. It was largely filled with rows of chairs. At one end on a dias stood a table topped with a hospital mattress covered in white rubber. On the wall behind the table was a blackboard bearing a line of chalk curlicues. Underneath was written in English: 'We can only ever heal ourselves, but sometimes we need to borrow another's hands – Swami Bopi Gul.' The other walls were hung with banners and devices with lamps burning beneath them. Some were holy pictures while others bore arcane symbols. One had a device of a white dove with outspread wings above a triangle containing an eye, with underneath the tag 'In Hoc Signo Vinci'. The first few rows of seats were mostly occupied. Altogether there were perhaps twenty-five people in the room. The Indian lady motioned for the Hemonys to sit.

The fat man was standing with his back to the room, facing what seemed to be a small shrine in one corner by the blackboard. Jason had the impression of a seated figurine lit by votive flames, surrounded by crimson silk embroidered with gold thread and flanked by smouldering joss-sticks. At the moment the *hadlam* appeared deep in prayer, holding in one hand a yellow tassel attached to the shrine in some way. The room settled into a long silence. Then the fat man turned and, still holding onto the tassel, began addressing his audience in dialect. It seemed to Tessa that he was speaking deliberately slowly to allow Sister Savitri time to translate for them.

'The *hadlam* is saying that he welcomes everyone, especially his foreign visitors who have come from so far. He says that Malomba is not the only place in the world having psychic healing. There are healers at all times and in every country. There are surgeons in other places, too, especially in the Philippines and South America. But Malomba is now the world centre for all the different healing disciplines gathered together.

'The *hadlam* says there is no reason for fear or embarrassment. A healer needs to have around him people who can give support to him and the patient. Healing concentration is very powerful. Everyone must to join hands and thinking of the colour blue, willing the sickness gone with all the love in your hearts. The greatest medicine is love.

'The *hadlam* adds that photography is allowed provided you ask the Spirit's permission first. Otherwise your camera may not work.'

Tapranne was now addressing the man in the sombrero who was sitting in the front row.

'He has been here before,' Sister Savitri told them. 'He

must to take off his hat and telling us what is the matter.'

The man got to his feet. Twenty-five pairs of eyes focused on the nail which gleamed in the strip-lighting.

'Always there is this pain in my head,' he explained. 'But sometimes it gets so bad I think it will explode like a bomb. I came two years ago and the *hadlam* used his powers. The headaches went away. Now they are as before and I am forced to put this nail in my head so when the pressure is too great I can take it out and let my brain breathe.'

There was a short buzz of conversation as the audience discussed these interesting symptoms.

'We didn't operate before,' Sister Savitri had Tapranne replying. 'I remember now, my friend. We used only magnetism to draw out this pressure. You are racing correspondent of the *Times of Malomba*, are you not? Known as the Golden Tipster? An intellectual gentleman. And there's the source of your trouble. Your work requires very rapid thinking, holding a lot of facts in your head. It's the pressure of your thought we're dealing with. Please come.' He motioned the man forward. 'Sit.' The Golden Tipster, still clutching his sombrero, walked his rump awkwardly up on to the edge of the mattress so that he was facing the audience. 'Join hands, please.' Sister Savitri extended a hand ostentatiously to Tessa on one side and to her neighbour on the other. From behind the *hadlam* two assistants approached. They looked like anyone at a stall in the Wednesday Market: a thirtyish man in T-shirt and rubber slippers and a woman holding a roll of lavatory paper.

The fat man adjusted his grass biretta and stared at the head of the nail. Slowly he reached out his hands, fingers outspread, until they hovered about an inch above it. Zoe and Jason watched, absorbed. Jason's sullenness had seemingly evaporated, to be replaced by fear as well as fascination. He held his sister's hand very tightly.

Still without touching the nail the *hadlam* asked, 'What do you feel, friend?'

'Cold, *hadlam*. The top of my head is cold.'

Tapranne lightly held the nail between the finger and thumb of one hand and gently withdrew it. Its tip glistened red. A sigh was heard in the room, as it might be of escaping air or maybe of an audience's indrawn breath. 'What do you feel, friend?'

'Still cold, *hadlam*.'

The fat man handed the nail to a helper and then placed both hands in a cupped gesture above his patient's head as if over a boil from which he was squeezing pus. Still he had not even touched the man's hair. Tapranne closed his eyes and flexed his knuckles as if kneading. From his patient's scalp appeared to rise a shiny black string like a wick or worm. The *hadlam* went on flexing. His watchers had the impression that his cupped palms were filling gradually with a wadded skein of this material, but the fingertips pointing down towards them hid any clear view. 'What do you feel, friend?'

'The top of my head's getting sort of light. It's like a cloud lifting. When will you take out the nail, *hadlam*?'

With a showman's gesture and still with his eyes closed, the fat man held up to his audience an indistinct tangle the size of a golf ball before dropping it in a plastic soup-plate his assistant extended. He made a gesture and the woman stepped forward, tearing off a handful of lavatory paper with which she dabbed at the patient's skull. Tapranne opened his eyes and gave off his beam. The whole process had taken barely three minutes.

'There, my friend. You've no more to worry about.' He put a hand on the man's shoulder and he looked nervously up, uncertain whether to smile. Tentatively he felt at his hair.

'*Hadlam-da, hadlam-da!*' he cried, face breaking into pleasure and relief. Needing no translation, this exclamation also marked a small catharsis for the audience, who smiled at each other and adjusted their fingers in one another's grip.

'There,' said Tessa. 'That wasn't very terrible, was it? As simple as that.'

'He's impressive,' said Zoe. 'You can feel his energy from here.'

'Can't you though? Great waves of it.'

Only Jason seemed less than wholly amazed. 'You can't see enough of what he's doing,' he objected. 'His hands weren't clear.'

'Oh come on, Jay,' said Tessa. 'How much more do you need to see? At the very least, a man came in with a headache and a nail and now he has neither.'

'I'm not surprised he had a headache with a piece of iron sticking in his brain. Probably the nail was quite loose anyway. I mean he's pretty good, though,' he said appeasingly, as if remembering that in a little while his own mother was going to be lying on the plastic mattress up front.

The Golden Tipster hopped down off the table and went out. His place was taken by a neatly dressed woman of about thirty-five who looked Chinese. A silence fell. Tapranne was back in the corner, stroking the yellow tassel as if milking it of power.

'Your name, my friend?' he asked briskly, returning centre-stage.

'I am Mrs Ling. I'm a businesswoman here in Malomba. The problem is in my stomach. Ever since my son died I'm head of the family company and the pains started. My doctor can find nothing wrong. The X-rays are negative. I suspect I'm being poisoned by a rival.'

The *hadlam* sidled around the edge of the table and caught up one of her hands. He peered closely into the woman's eyes, had her swing her legs up, examined the backs of both knees.

'It's much more serious than poison,' he announced. 'But don't be afraid. We can help you.'

'Is it cancer then, *hadlam*?'

'No, worse.' He turned to face the audience once more.

134

'My friends, I need all your help now. This lady is a victim of witchcraft. An evil has been put into her which we must remove. Don't imagine' – and here he seemed to be speaking more to his foreign guests – 'that because a spell is put on it doesn't have a real and actual counterpart. Evil can take a physical form, of course.'

Meanwhile his helpers were inducing Mrs Ling to lie full length on the plastic mattress. Her blouse was pulled up so that the lower part of her breasts was visible, while her skirt was opened to reveal the elastic waistband of severe black lingerie; this was pushed lower until her entire midriff lay pale and bare under the light. Tapranne moved behind the table and gazed earnestly at a point on the ceiling. The woman closed her eyes. Meanwhile the male helper had himself gone to the corner and milked the tassel, now returning to hover behind Tapranne, rubbing his hands together constantly and flicking invisible drops of spiritual energy at the healer's back.

The fat man momentarily spread all his fingers very wide, then tented each hand so that the tips of his fingers came together in two separate bunches. He then seemed to push these bunches with some difficulty through the skin of Mrs Ling's stomach. Crimson liquid gleamed between his fingers. The patient maintained an expression of unwitting serenity while the fat man's lips parted in a kind of snarl. There was a faint but distinct splashing sound. He grunted some words with effort. His assistant behind him rubbed and flicked, rubbed and flicked.

'It's fighting us,' whispered Sister Savitri. 'Think of blue. Think of healing. Think of the Master's words, that we are in Bliss where such things can have no power. Men may misuse the power of the mind for their own gain, but such stupidities and dross must eventually yield and fall away before the power of love.' Zoe recognised the quotation and tightened her grip.

'Yes!' cried Tapranne suddenly, his hay cap askew. 'Yes!'

135

His hands were now covered in scarlet and the lady with the lavatory paper was swabbing at Mrs Ling's white flank. 'Its power is dead. Its power is dead! Its power is DEAD!' and with a flourish which matched his shout he held triumphantly up in one hand a curly object a couple of inches long. There was a gasp of horror from the front rows.

'Oh, what is it?' cried Jason. 'I can't see.'

The *hadlam* tossed the thing into the plastic soup-plate and his fingers returned to the apparent deep wound in Mrs Ling's stomach. Then he stepped back. His male helper handed him a cloth while the woman with the lavatory roll cleaned off the site of the operation.

'That was not easy,' the healer told his audience, wiping his hands and still breathing hard. 'I felt opposition from some of you out there. A few negative vibrations.' Jason shrank in his seat and swallowed. 'Come, see for yourselves.' He raised a hand and beckoned.

They all rose and pressed forward to the dais. The first thing Jason noticed when he got close to the table was the smell of blood, thick and tinny. Fearfully he glanced at Mrs Ling, then looked properly. Apart from a faint redness on her skin as after a light punch, together with a certain puckering, there was not the least sign of a wound. On the plastic dish lay a dying scorpion in a red puddle. Even as he watched, its legs ticked into their last folding. He looked back at the stomach and didn't know what to think. Instead, he noticed a few uppermost strands of pubic hair disappearing beneath her waistband. He glanced away in embarrassment for her exactly at the moment when *hadlam* Tapranne put his hand lightly on her forehead and said a few words. She opened her eyes and sat up, examining her own flesh with satisfied awe as if it were an expensive new acquisition. Then, realising it was also being goggled at by many pairs of strange eyes gathered around, she at once tugged down her blouse. That was when she caught sight of the scorpion. Her cry was part hiss, part yelp.

But the *hadlam* had turned and was already greeting Tessa in English. He had removed his biretta, which looked to be woven of hay so fresh it was still pale green.

'And your children too. Swami Gul told me all, of course. The beautiful daughter. Charming.' Sweat twinkled at his hair roots. The teeth again. 'Our backache has been with us for years, yes? On and off, on and off. I see I see.'

'Never completely off. Until the last two or three days, *hadlam*.'

'I see I see. As of this moment you have no pain?' He rested a fingertip on the nape of her neck. 'Nothing?'

'Nothing, *hadlam*.'

'Interesting. I detect a definite imbalance. We must look at your soles; they will infallibly tell the rest of the story. Up on the table, please. Your children will stay and hold your hands. Innocence and love are most potent forces for healing.'

The fat man's eye briefly met Jason's and at that moment the boy saw how he had been enmeshed. He couldn't refuse. On the other hand, if despite his best intentions his influence turned out to be 'negative' he would be endangering his mother's chances of recovery. Glumly he recognised he would have to take the responsibility if her cure failed, since it was clear the people in this room would rather die than think of blaming the *hadlam*. Sister Savitri had meanwhile waved the others back to their seats while remaining on the stage as interpreter. Tapranne passed his hand over Tessa's naked soles, never closer to them than half an inch. From time to time he made flicking motions with his fingers as if to shake off drops of some invisible ichor.

'I see I see. Strange indeed you should be experiencing no discomfort in your spine as of these days. There is a long-standing defect and a blockage which has recently grown acute. The last half-year it has become worse? Yes. Your soles cannot lie. The beautiful blouse off please, Mrs Hemony.'

Jason stared at Sister Savitri's nose bead until his mother was lying naked to the waist, face down on the pudgy plastic. There was a mole on one shoulder-blade which was both familiar and poignant. He watched the *hadlam*'s hands move slowly over her skin. They stopped like dog muzzles on her lower spine.

'I see I see. Your problem is an *over-abundance*.' Sister Savitri passed on this news to the audience. 'One tiny part too many which throws the whole body out of that perfect balance we aim for. Yes. Look at the blackboard, my young man. What does it say?'

It took Jason a moment to realise he was being addressed. He could feel himself blushing as he turned and read off the sentence in English.

'Exactly,' the fat man said. 'We must heal ourselves but sometimes we need help. A paradox, yes?'

Jason found himself watching a loose wisp of hay on the man's cap and only then knew he was averting his eyes from the bunched fingers to all appearance now deep in a scarlet pit in his mother's back. The clasp of her hand and his was in marble.

'Do you like paradox, my young man?' He thought he could smell her blood now and once more hear a distinct and miniature splashing. 'I see I see. Swami Gul does, too. He has a playfulness which is the mark of the divine. You too are in the grip of a paradox. I can feel you. Yes. You do not really believe this is happening, yet you can see what you can see. Also smell and hear. So, do you wish to put your hand here? Well? Do you not want evidence?' And the hay cap rotated backwards and the *hadlam*'s great round face came up into his. Bloody fingers were held before the teeth, in their tips a roughly circular piece of pinkish gristle. For an atrocious moment Jason thought Tapranne was going to reach out and force his fingers into the wound below, but the expression in the healer's eyes was mischievous, not sadistic.

'So it's all in the mind, is it, my young man? After all?' The assistant with the lavatory paper was swabbing away at Tessa's back. There was no wound. Jason knew his attention had been distracted by the lump of gristle, so he had not seen what the other hand was doing. Two vivid minutes stood revealed as having been smudged with talk. 'Strange how the brain controls the brain,' Tapranne was babbling on. 'Who said that, my young man?'

'The Teacher,' Jason replied mechanically.

'Wrong!' cried the *hadlam*. 'Not Gul at all but Sherlock Holmes.'

The gristle was in the soup-plate, his mother was doing up her blouse, her eyes never leaving Tapranne's face. Jason was suddenly in vast disgust and let go of her hand. The smell, the fat man's sweat, the blood and gristle, the audience, the muddle of it. Nothing was clear, nor ever would be – the entrancement on his mother's face least of all. He made for the door, forcing the others to follow. In the passageway outside he caught Sister Savitri's voice behind saying, 'A contribution, Sister? Though only if you want,' and heard his mother rustling in her Tibetan bag. Through the conservatory, elbowing aside the halt and the maimed and the blind, the goitred, tumoured, ulcerated, leaking, prolapsed throng, the handful of dilettante sick and the unabashed groupies, and out into raw Malombian sunshine where bored drivers tossed coins in the dust.

When Tessa and Zoe caught up with him he expected his mother to say, 'But Jay, it was you who insisted on coming,' and was angry when she failed to give him this chance to be angry. Instead he said, '*Now* can we go home? Are you happy *now?*'

Suppertime again.

Sweet intestine, Laki's favourite. He reached into the pot with paint-stained fingers and hooked out a pale, springy length. Putting one end in his mouth, he sucked out the contents until the pipe whistled thinly.

'They'll be leaving soon.'

'How do you know?'

'I'm painting the passage outside her room, uncle. I heard them talking. Also the boy came up to the roof this afternoon.'

'No guests allowed on the roof, boy. You're playing with fire.'

'What if the fire comes to be played with, uncle?' Laki snapped off a piece of tubing and thought of Jason's *kancha* practice. The boy had been oblivious to all implorings to be careful, wandering the roof in broad daylight and sending down a manic hail of projectiles in all directions. He had hit a deer and given a shout of triumph as the beast had bolted into the shrubbery. Finally he had loosed a chunk of mud down into the street, hitting a cart and sending a spray of stinging particles among the crowds in front of the BDL. Faint cries had come up; Laki had dragged Jason below the parapet and snatched away the catapult. The boy had collapsed on the mat in the hutch, almost tearful but falling instead into a familar evacuated drowse. Heat, *karesh* flowers; adrift in a mud room. Once again Jason had given himself up to a secret no longer secret, a way of wrenching a small piece of time out of gear until he could coast in silence, gradually losing speed.

'What are you doing to us?' he had asked finally, up on one elbow.

'I only bell-boy.'

'You're doing something, I know you are.' The T-shirt trembled to his heart. The rest of his clothes were moulted on the floor like fragments of an epidermis now outgrown.

And just then Laki had seen how it was with people who

secretly wanted things to happen. They knew themselves immune and had to live in a permanent state of bafflement. Everything came as a surprise. Nothing had a shape until afterwards. Belatedly he glimpsed how difficult it truly might be to forge links of obligation with people so far removed from the hard-edged world he knew. What was the equivalent in the Hemonys' life of the engine which would transform his father's fishing overnight? What recurrent calamity might force them to eat badly for a month? Nothing was clear about them. But that was not to say they were shifty. One could spot shiftiness at a thousand paces by the way it smiled. The Hemonys were quite the reverse: they seemed to live entirely in the open, naked and undefended to the point of embarrassment. Yet they managed to be wholly visible without the least clarity. How did they do it? And thinking of the marine engine pushed his mind into that circle which led to foreigners with wealth to spare, which in turn led him back to the Hemonys and how inscrutable they were, how impossibly *other*, how hopeless his plans. Still, one would persevere.

'All the same it's playing with fire, boy. Muffy's got it in for you.'

'Oh? Of course, the toddy. It's a pity about that, uncle. Getting caught was sheer bad luck. How was I to know the old bugger would be hanging about the yard at that time of evening? He ought to have been long since at home with that crone of his.'

Raju winced and looked nervously behind him. The kitchen at his back held nothing more menacing than a cook, sooty cobwebs, clouds of grease and some sleepy hens in the rafters. 'Your tongue, boy; you must learn to hold it. It'll be the death of you. Remember the mouse which slept in the cat's ear? A nice comfortable billet demands subtlety and discretion, especially when the cat's got its claws out. It's not just the toddy. He hates everything about you just now; he's jealous.'

'Of me, uncle?'

'Certainly, boy. I've seen his face. You get on too well with these foreigners. The girl smiles at you.'

'What's a smile, uncle?' (But the excitement of hearing it!)

'There are smiles and smiles . . . How dense you are. But how very young, I suppose. You can't know what it would mean to a man Muffy's age if a beautiful blonde foreign girl smiled at him like that. Believe me, I know,' said Raju sadly, 'only too well. He and I are the same age. Just never let him see you doing your grinning capers. No need to keep poking the bruise. They'll have gone in a day or two. That's my advice, boy. Stick to your duties. Answer bells. Paint. Plenty of other foreign fish for your net.'

'Until there's a Red Tide, uncle. Any more troubles, any more freedom fighters, any more MNLP or whatever it's called, and there'll be a shortage.'

'Sooner or later they'll come back, boy. Red Tides always move on. Malomba's a holy city . . .'

'I'd better take some pictures of it now I'm here. I s'pose,' Jason had said before going back down, and produced a small Canon. He pointed it all over the townscape, especially at the Glass Minaret and the surly, stepped pile of the Lingasumin. 'My friends in Italy won't believe there's a church where they actually screw during services.' In between pictures the camera whirred and wheezed.

They had taken pictures of each other, Laki posed against the vine rather self-consciously holding his *kancha*.

'Very beautiful camera.'

''s all right.'

'You make pictures to the *hadlam*?'

'No, I forgot to take it. Anyway I wouldn't have.'

'He to healing your sister?'

'It was my *mother*,' Jason had rounded on him. 'Can't you understand that? Don't you ever listen? It was my *mother*'s back. He pretended to take something out. Or maybe he really did. I don't know anything about it. Probably it was all just a trick. Conjuring. Magic. It's a mess. It's all a mess.'

'I'm not believing, I think,' ventured Laki. Maybe this boy actually shared some of his own surprise at the incoherence of their lives. At least his sister hadn't been the patient. The golden princess was no invalid after all.

'A mess,' Jason was repeating. He blinked angrily at the foothills in the afternoon light. Already shadows were beginning to form in their folds. 'She's been up here, hasn't she?'

'Never come here,' said Laki.

'Yes, she has. I've heard her voice in the night. I'm in that shitty room right below here, remember?' He stamped a foot near the crack through which the laundry water ran. Only then did Laki realise this foreign boy was still not talking about his beautiful blonde sister. 'So what *are* you doing to us?'

'You'll help me though, uncle, won't you?' Laki asked, licking at a skein of mesentery wrapped around his fingers.

'Help you cut your own throat? I suppose so. But I shan't go out of my way.'

'Just keep me informed, uncle. That's all.'

But there was little for Raju to pass on an hour or so later when Laki went out to play the pinball machines with his friend from the bakery. The Hemonys had apparently returned from an early supper, the woman and the boy looking especially tired. Laki put them out of his mind in the search for his friend, who was not at home. Doubling back towards the squalid amusement hall, he crossed the road near the Nirvana just in time to see Zoe leave it. She had changed out of her T-shirt and grubby jeans and was wearing a blouse and an airy cotton skirt long enough to appease Malomba's sensibilities and short enough to tighten his chest. Friend and slot machines instantly forgotten, he followed at a careful distance the ingot of her hair which flashed as she passed the doorways of shops and merchants.

143

He knew where she was heading even before she left Justice and turned into Sobriety. This was no evening stroll. Her walk was purposeful and she didn't hesitate when she reached the junction with Awareness. From the end of that street could be heard the steady thudding of rock music, and it seemed to him the blackened windows of The Punk Panther were themselves like drumskins, alternately denting and bulging to the concussions within. Her hair caught violet fire as she opened its door and vanished inside. A waft of decibels rolled up the street.

One reached the rear of The Punk Panther – if one were a bell-boy accustomed to climbing palm trees daily – by squeezing down a urine-sodden passage several doors away. This was less an alley than an eighteen-inch error in surveying, left over between an ice merchant's and the Mother Lily Mission. Laki had once done some moonlighting at the Mission's ramshackle premises, stacking cardboard boxes of exhortatory booklets. He knew little enough about Mother Lily herself except that she would never allow the phrase 'sinner' to be used, referring only to 'persons of restricted moral growth'. He knew rather more about her back yard and the disposition of its heaps of junk, the rusting bedsteads and piles of donated clothing bursting out of rotten crates. This knowledge now served him well, enabling him once over the wall to make a series of athletic moves. He scaled a sodden alp of jerseys, slipping on a crop of toadstools near the summit but finding his balance enough to take off from one foot and reach an overhanging branch.

In this manner he neared the area ahead which pulsed din and flashes of light up into the sky. The Punk Panther's back premises were known generically as a Beer Garden, as if an enchanted offspring might come of the union of two unassuming nouns. It remained a back yard, although filled with potted ferns between high walls covered in creepers. Its far end resembled the Nirvana's rear, in that behind thick shrubbery was a fence of bamboo staves. Beyond that lay a pocket wilderness. Laki made his way around this end and in through the fence, sidling up between bushes. As an under-age Malomban he was not allowed into any sort of night club: even kitchen staff were supposed by statute to be over eighteen. This being Malomba, however, a ten-year leeway was observed where menials were concerned and Laki had several friends here who worked as washers-up, beer-crate heavers and assorted touts crouched in the shadows looking for prey. Tonight, in any case, he could approach the club with the inward swagger of one who had proved himself with a woman, and a blonde foreign woman at that. He definitely felt entitled to put on a casual air in a den of international vice, though he knew it was no guarantee against detection by the proprietor, a violent Australian.

For all the noise and frenzied strobe lights, there were only fifteen or twenty foreigners sitting inside at fibreglass tables moulded to represent mushrooms. In between blazes of colour the room reverted to its basic pitch dark lit only by a handful of candles and the console lights of the sound system. Any activity was frozen into a series of movie frames. Violet hands jerked through the air. The only still object seemed to be the cat, Snort, whose intermittent outline Laki could see in his favourite place on top of the stack of amplifiers. Snort was famous, not just in Malomba but among travellers and backpackers from Sydney to San Francisco. He was stone-deaf after years of The Punk Panther's night life and had frequently had his furry wits scrambled by *sima* which the unscrupulous fed him in rolled anchovies. At such moments he would dash about outside, banging into trees. Now he was aloof in his electronic high-rise; his earring winked as he dozed.

It took Laki a minute to spot Zoe, sitting by herself at a table in the corner. Expressions were unreadable in the flickering gloom, but her arm jerked towards her face from time to time as she looked at her watch. It was a nervous gesture, touchingly out of place. Time was meaningless in The Punk Panther. Sooner or later, Laki knew, she would be approached and drawn into the main body of zonked expatriates. Already she had been spotted by the club's hospitality machine; a tall glass stood before her. In a momentary respite between two soundtracks, a hollow grinding squeak could be heard and a sawn-off creature scuttered toward her mushroom. It nodded and rowed like a toy in a tin boat, its head scooting between legs and stalks. Zoe's face jerked down to the sinister whirl at the hem of her skirt. Twin appendages reached up to her from nether darkness.

Laki slid unobserved into the kitchen. 'There's a girl sitting alone in the corner by the beer ad.,' he said to Gusa. 'Vippu's just getting his claws into her. Five *piku* to bring her out to the garden. Tell her it's . . . no, just tell her it's a friend and it's very urgent.'

The girl – whose job description was variously hostess, waitress and burlesque dancer – bared the gap left by an eye-tooth. '*Now* what are we up to, Laki-boy?' she asked without much curiosity, tucking the coin into a pocket. 'Wait outside. Don't let the owner see you here; he's pissed-off enough as it is. This place is becoming a morgue.'

On his way out to the verandah Laki passed an un-occupied mushroom. In its red domed top were irregular white recesses: maggot-holes for standing drinks, ashtrays and so on. Into the centre, as into that of all the others, was let a plastic bowl. This contained the black boiled sweets which were as widely famed as old Snort himself. Distri-buted free to the club's customers, they were available only in blackcurrant flavour and were supposed to offset the side-effects of something or other. Laki helped himself liberally from the bowl, cramming the sweets into his pockets as he went outside to lurk in the bushes. After quite a wait Zoe came out, looking apprehensively around. He met her briskly, for he had already worked out his story.

'Lucky!' she exclaimed. To his fond ears, at least, she sounded relieved to see him.

'Oh miss. Very bad. You must to come now.'

'What's happened? It's not my mother?'

'No, no, miss. Not that. But you know I have many friends in Malomba, hear many things. Tonight, now!, are coming police to this club. Many drug here, many bad criminal. Police to arresting all foreigners maybe and to beating perhaps. Or to raping,' he added judiciously, watching her face for effect.

'But I've not done—'

He stabbed a finger at her fist, surprising her by the violence of the gesture. It was the first time he had touched her. 'You are to buying *sima* from Vippu. Very bad boy, police catch many times. Maybe this time they to killing him. I watch you buy,' he said slyly.

Bewildered as intended by this revelation of raw Third World menace behind what had been for her a daring attempt at time off, Zoe became almost paralysed with ordinary fear. No one knew she was here; anything might happen to her. All notions of divine protection evaporated. She was fifteen and alone on the edges of the underworld in a remote part of the planet – alone, that is, but for a single familiar face turned earnestly up into hers.

'You are to eating *sima*?'

'No, no.' This was untrue. Spellbound by its seller's beautiful malignity, Zoe had in fact taken a cautious nibble at Vippu's urging in the hope that it might make her more relaxed and open to enjoyment. She had been startled at first by the drug's bitterness, then intrigued enough by its aromatic, fudgelike texture to try another sample. Now she squeezed the pellet she held so as to obliterate her teeth-marks.

'Come, you give,' Laki thrust out his hand. 'So police not find to you.' She gave it up. Instead of throwing it away he

147

slipped it into his own pocket with a capable gesture which said he would take care of everything. Next he had taken her hand and was tugging it towards the bushes. Sensing her resistance, he urged: 'Quick. Police they come in front. We to go out back, miss.'

And in that moment the *sima* hit her and she saw with extraordinary clarity the boy's brown fingers around hers, heard the pounding drums behind them and pushing them away from the club, outwards into soft Malomban night. Exhilaration poured into the hole left by fear, filling her up with a skittish helium as she floated through the shrubbery behind her marvellous friend. An adventure was beginning. Away from the virtuous rigours of Valcognano, beyond the reach of gurus and healers and Elders, she was young at last in the company of the young.

There began a singular journey in which she merrily fled a menace that grew ever more indistinct behind them. Following Laki through undergrowth whose coils and tangles seemed magically to melt, she found herself on a street where people and vehicles moved in slow motion to a low murmur of sound while a keen whistle of breeze sped by her ears. Merchants were putting up their shutters as if drowning in treacle, a viscid gold medium which parted to let her through and then closed behind her whizzing heels.

'Oh Lucky!' she cried, her hair flying. But he was pulling her to a halt at the corner of Justice.

Laki had had some vague plan of spiriting her up to his eyrie on the hotel roof, but now as he looked along at the front entrance it struck him that the girl's wretched mother might inconveniently take it into her head to make the same journey. The moment was resolved by Zoe herself saying, 'Don't let's go back to that smelly old hotel yet. I want to do something mad.'

'Mad, miss?'

'Pretty mad.'

'Okay miss. I take somewhere. But must to go behind Nirbana.'

He led her along the street praying nobody would come out of the hotel, at last ducking down the strip of waste ground which ran at the side of the building. They squelched past the fallen sheet of corrugated iron which overflowing water bonged each dawn, over a wall of decaying hollow blocks, across the back yard and into the bananas. Once there Laki guided her along his toddy-gathering trail until they were standing hand in hand, breathless on the edge of the Redemptorist Fathers' greensward with the little pagoda shimmering before them in the light of a full, tropic moon. Immediately there was a sharp hissing and a rocket rushed up the sky and burst into a crimson canopy of tumbling lights, then into a second and even larger blue umbrella above that, leaving a huge jellyfish drifting earthwards shedding filaments and sparks.

'Ooh, is that for us?'

'Of course,' he told her opportunistically, squeezing her hand. In fact it merely meant it was ten thirty-five, the official Kalustrian midnight when at the full moon the tortured god Kalu begged for a firebrand with which to cauterise the ninety-nine wounds inflicted on him by an uncaring human race. This stark remedy his devotees sent him monthly was intended to keep him so occupied with self-surgery he would have no time for vengeance. Thus global doom was kept at bay for the mere cost of a dozen 'Chrysanthemum' brand Chinese rockets a year – according to the Kalustrian community, a pretty shrewd investment.

'I know where this is,' she was saying in surprise, for time was getting out of sequence and turning their flight into a directionless escapade. It was fun, though. 'We're in that garden.'

'We safe here in case police to searching hotel.'

This made good sense to Zoe, at least. By the light of the

moon and with the blotches of the Kalustrians' rocket still on her retinas, the Fathers' garden seemed a magic haven, an enchanted playground. She ran about the lawn for a while trying to catch fireflies. Laki followed anxiously, urging her not to make too much noise. Whatever might be about to fall into his hands was too precious to risk. He recognised her symptoms and wondered how much *sima* she had really eaten. Impossible to estimate from the lump in his pocket, since Vippu would certainly have cheated her. She skipped over the little bridge and into the pagoda. Following, he found her sprawled on one of the benches.

'Oh miss, we not to staying here.'

'Why not? It's a pretty little house. Let's live here, just you and me. I'm afraid we can't get married, of course; you're just a child . . . Why do all the cracks here have sparks in them? It's such a lovely idea.'

Mildly slighted, he could hardly tell the missus's own daughter how unjustified her accusation was. Just a child, indeed. The cohabitation theme, though, was far more what he wanted to hear. 'We must to live upstairs, miss. The Fathers are using this room sometimes. We must to live in secret.'

'Even better. But how do we get upstairs?'

'Climbing, miss. I have room upstairs. I show if we climb.'

She sat up. 'Climb? That's a great idea. You any good at climbing?'

'I to climbing palm trees. Very quick.'

'Where I live in Italy there's a lot of wet chestnut trees and a sort of mountain. There isn't anything worth climbing. But here . . .' She sprang up and went outside. The pagoda sparkled in the moonlight like a tiered wedding-cake. 'It's so romantic. It's perfect. Bit thirsty, though, that's the only thing.' And before he could stop her she threw herself down by the bridge like some Pre-Raphaelite shepherd boy and drank deeply from the midge-mantled sump. 'Wow! That's good . . . If,' she stood back, hands on hips, looking up at the pagoda, 'if at last I'm going to do something crazy, we're going to do it in style. Take off your clothes.'

So intent had Laki been on playing rescuer and guide that he hadn't seen how imperceptibly their roles were switching. This bizarre command made him abruptly aware of how much – now that she was on his ground – he wanted to do her bidding. Her gold ingot of hair hung down in the moonlight as earnest of a vast treasure which might be possessed in its entirety if only one knew the map or the password or had the right key. With infinite luck a lifetime's bullion lay to hand.

'To taking off clothes, miss?'

'Sure. I've had an idea, dear heart.' (*Dear heart!*) 'It's bliss. You and I are going to swap clothes.'

'Miss?'

'Don't you see? I'll wear your clothes and you'll wear mine. Just for fun, while we're climbing. That way, if anybody comes they'll never know it's us. I'll be you and you'll be me. No Father's going to be bright enough to see through that. Come on.' She pulled off her blouse. 'You shy or something? It's only for a laugh. We're like brother and sister, you and me.'

Confused by this casual enactment of his wildest fantasy, Laki could only pluck feebly at his own T-shirt. She held out her hand imperiously for it, offering her blouse in the other. Lowering his eyes shyly from her breasts, he slowly pulled it over his head.

'Now your shorts,' she said relentlessly. 'It's a good job we're the same size. I may as well tell you I'm not wearing anything underneath this dress. Girls often don't on really hot evenings. There: you've learned something about women I bet you didn't know. Don't just stand . . . Oh, I've got it. You're embarrassed to wear girls' clothes. Your precious manhood and all that. Too bad. Either we're properly mad or I'm going back to the hotel.' She jumped lightly on to the flimsy stone balustrade of the bridge and walked along it dressed simply in his T-shirt, her arms held out on either side and very white. Within a minute or two she was wearing his shorts and examining him critically as he stood there in her blouse and skirt. She walked all around him.

'You're perfect,' she told him. 'Seriously perfect.' But he was still too abashed to say anything, so she took his hand and pulled him towards the pagoda. 'Come on, now, show me. What's the best way of getting up this thing?'

'Here, miss.' He indicated a gnarled stirrup of vine stem.

'You can't call me miss. You must call me mister. Okay, miss?'

'Yes, mister,' came a reluctant voice.

She giggled a bit, but soon became intent on following his swaying skirts as he went from handhold to handhold with practised agility.

'This my room,' he called down.

'Higher. I want to go right to the top.'

As they climbed, fragments of decaying concrete broke off like icing sugar and pattered down through the leaves below. Soon they reached the point where the pagoda was so slender that Zoe could put her arms right round it. She stood with her feet in one of the window embrasures of the topmost cell and looked about her with dizzy pleasure.

'What are those lights, miss?' she asked.

'That our Nirbana Hotel.'

She thought of her mother and brother sleeping or reading behind their respective lit windows. They seemed as remote as if she were watching the rows of lighted portholes in a liner's side as it passed and wondering who the unknown passengers were. People on a journey. Soon she would herself be going to California; she had just decided. 'What about those others?'

'Redemptorist Fathers, miss . . . er, mister.' Through the gauzy billows of the cloud-tree shone yellowish lamplight at an indeterminate distance. 'I think we to come down. It very danger here. No good this cement.'

'Oh, you're no fun.' But she began backing down the vertiginous spire. On the first storey she found him already inside his chamber. He had lit a candle and a mosquito coil was smouldering beside an open box. 'What a sweet place,' she said, squeezing in through a window. 'Only the ceiling's a bit low.' She dropped to all fours. 'Golly, a carpet, no less. You've got yourself really set up, haven't you? And flowers coming in the window, too.'

Crouched opposite her almost knee to knee, he smiled doubtfully. Things had got a little beyond him. Eyes and teeth twinkled in the candlelight. She reached out and touched the tip of his nose.

'Poor Miss Lucky. You look so baffled and pretty; you should just see yourself.' For as he knelt the dress came down around him in the most demure way. Only the brown arms emerging from the narrow blouse seemed too sinewy. 'But you're not quite complete.' She slipped a bracelet from her wrist on to his. It was of twined copper and silver, hammered flat and set with peridot and zircon. Swami Bopi Gul himself had given it her and it had some magical or curative significance. The design was striking, but she always thought it lay on an uneasy borderline between adornment and therapeutics. The boy was evidently pleased with the effect, though, turning it round and round so the candlelight flared the stones. 'There,' said Zoe. 'Now you're perfect. You look quite unspoilt.'

To her eyes the entire room was now glittering as if sequins had been mixed in with the mortar. The drug's manic effects had peaked. Unknown to her, she was entering a phase where mild visual disturbance would turn into acute tactile sensitivity and then to drowsiness. Later would come the headache. She lay full length on the carpet and rolled experimentally on its mildewed softness. The scent of *karesh* blossom was heavy in the night air.

153

'What on earth have you got in your pockets?' She pulled out handfuls of black sweets. 'I'm going to tell you the story of my life,' she said, crunching blackcurrant while holding up the wrapper so that its crinkles sent out prismatic flares which hurt her eyes. 'I was born and years and years passed and my father ran off and I took a lover from California. He was American of course, incredibly rich and handsome. I used to visit him in LA – that's Los Angeles – and we'd drive around Hollywood in this Cadillac of his which had a bar and a telephone and everything. Ed – that's this American – told me I was quite unspoilt and that I had to get away from my family if only because my mother's a bit loopy. We would live in . . . in Bel Air, in a huge mansion he had with Mexican maids and an English butler. The butler's name was Ponkerton, actually. Marriage was discussed, of course, but it was decided he was still a little immature and we agreed on a trial period.

'And then one day he came back from the studios and poured himself a big drink and lit a Chesterfield and walked round and round the room. The poor darling looked so upset I asked him what the matter was, and he said it was the most terrible news and I must brace myself for a shock. The doctor had told him he had an incurable disease. He meant cancer, of course, not AIDS. It was like a knife in my heart, as you can imagine. It didn't seem possible. He was so young and handsome and our lives were before us.

'Of course we tried everything. We must have gone to every doctor in Hollywood, but the diagnosis was always the same: Ed would die in months. So then I thought of this man I know – he's a famous guru called Swami Bopi Gul. If anyone could heal Ed surely he could. So the Swami tried all he knew, but it made no difference. If anything it actually made him worse. Finally we took him for radium therapy and all his beautiful hair fell out. You should have seen him, he looked ghastly. Just bones, really, and this waxy yellow skin.

'Well naturally he died, right there in his Bel Air mansion, and Ponkerton came out into the garden where I was cutting flowers for his bedside and said, "The master has left us, Miss Zoe. It was better this way." I rushed upstairs and there he was and I threw myself on to the bed and wept and kissed his lifeless face and laid the flowers on his breast. Later we buried him in Mount . . . Monterey, in a quiet churchyard overlooking the sea. And ever since then I suppose I've been trying to put him out of my mind. It's been hard, but I think now at last I'm free of his memory.'

Zoe lay chewing stoically, the tears her own story had induced running back into her hairline. Beside her, eyes wide on hers, Laki was also crunching away. The carpet around them was littered with wrappers. Much of the story's detail had been lost on him, but he was left with an absolute conviction of the princess-like quality of the girl on the floor. California . . . servants . . . doctors . . . death: more than enough to suggest a tragic fairytale life of elsewhere. That world really did exist, far, far from Malomba, where everyone did what they felt like and money was never mentioned. This lovely high blonde girl now wearing his own tatty shorts was herself a denizen of that life, a mysterious fragment broken off a distant slab of glamour and washed up on to his doorstep. He ran his hands wonderingly over the blouse and the dress, examined the bracelet on his own wrist, then looked down at her. His T-shirt had never appeared so unfamiliar, for all that he knew every hole. Ordinarily its faded slogan in green Gothic lettering – 'The Bank of the Divine Lotus. Where Purity Meets Security' – lay flat across his chest. Now the letters were distorted and a stretch-wrinkle ran through the logo of a padlocked lotus.

'I can feel your eyes.'

He put out a fingertip and touched the lotus. It was suspended in air. 'I want to coming with you to Italy. Possible?'

'Of course you must come. But I warn you it's quite mad and boring. You must come dressed as you are. Little Miss Lucky.' She reached up and sank her fingers into his hair. 'Asian hair. Glossy wire. Full of . . . you're full of electricity, you know that? I can see your sparkles.'

'Yes, Miss Zoe.'

'Mister. Mister. *Mister*,' and the third time jerked his head downwards so abruptly that he was dragged off balance and had to kneel across her to remain upright. Straightening against her pull, he hit the back of his head on the ceiling. One of his bare feet kicked the candle over; hot wax spilled across it. In the darkness something began moving beneath the dress. 'Rotten cheat,' she said. 'You left your underpants on. I don't call that fair . . . Oh, the smell of these flowers. They do something to your brain, you know that?'

'Wait, mister, I to lighting candle.' Laki tried to lever himself away from her hands, the whole delicious indignity of it. All was confused. Not one single thing was clear, least of all with nothing but silvery moonlight leaking in through the six thin windows. He himself no longer knew what he wanted. These people had the power to whirl things about until something happened, it semed not to matter what. Her hands were running like mice at play, meanwhile. 'Wait, mister,' he began again, then fell suddenly dumb. From the garden below came the sound of a voice, two voices, above the racket of frogs.

'Lucky . . .'

'Ssh, miss, Father McGoohan to coming here.' He was still trying to pull free. 'Oh please miss, no noise. Very bad if he to catching us.'

The voices neared and Zoe became silent but didn't relax her grip. The bell-boy was left kneeling over her, a leg on either side, while she pulled more and more of his weight downwards on to her stomach. As her eyes adjusted she began to see his face above her, washed in moonlight, balanced like a flower on the ruffed collar of her blouse. The vine exhaled.

'. . . have ears,' came Father McGoohan's voice from downstairs, 'which is why some things are better said far from the madding crowd. Twenty years in this country have convinced me that you can't be too careful. We're here on sufferance. There's almost nothing you can say which won't be construed as a political statement. You'll have to be on your guard up-country.'

'Ssh,' said Zoe, and giggled softly.

'. . . may have told you that in Dublin but believe me, things are pretty different on the ground here.' The smell of a freshly-lit pipe.

Laki tried to catch her hands beneath the cotton, to grip them imploringly.

'. . . find Malomba itself genially antinomian. So many books of scripture there's no room left for ordinary moral law. "Right" and "wrong" don't seem to mean much unless you cite an authority, and since there are at least thirty different religious authorities here it puts one in an interesting position, theologically. Especially now, in Holy Week.'

On her back Zoe was drawing her bare feet towards her over the carpet, pushing up her knees.

'. . . to live up to our famous austere standards. You'll find one of our major problems is distribution. Simply no infrastructure to speak of.'

The pressure of her thighs was forcing Laki to shuffle forward on his knees.

'The Palace is absolutely paranoid. The whole horrible charade will have to be played out, of course, heaps of bodies and all. The usual vile escalation. More repression, more MNLP, more special forces, more people's retribution squads, more gangs of police in mufti licensed to shoot on sight . . .'

To save his balance Laki had eventually to sit right

forward on her chest, trapped between wall and ceiling, hands outstretched to the windowsill, bangle gleaming.

'. . . of course not. Never forget, the family's everything here. You're a cabinet minister, and you screw everyone left and right including Central Government funds and walk away with the loot to Switzerland or the Cayman Islands and secretly everyone'll be saying, "Right on. The better for his family. Wish it could've been me."'

Now the dress was spread out around him, hiding her to the hips. Her head had vanished and with it the entire bright pool of her hair. The moonlight ran off the material in all directions as if it were a marquee pitched and waiting in a secret wood.

'. . . liberation theology . . .'

From within the marquee came the smallest sounds imaginable, mice nibbling.

'. . . corruption . . .'

He gave an involuntary sigh, elbow thudding into the wall. A dreadful silence.

'Just monkeys,' said Father McGoohan. 'Thing is not to get paranoid oneself.'

Altogether, he and his companion spent another hour and three-quarters in earnest conversation, their pipe smoking drifting up through the window slits and mingling with the scent of the vine. During all that time only two words were spoken in the room above, when she pulled his face to hers by the hair and said with blackcurrant breath: *'Mister* Lucky.'

Ong Mokpin was late for his appointment and Tessa, waiting in the Golden Fortune's Waikiki Bar, ordered a second Hawaiian punch. It arrived with a good deal of supplementary flotsam and litter: vague green slices, pineapple pulp, orange sticks, paper umbrellas. One way and another she was glad to be leaving Malomba. More and more she felt she'd been selfish. Her back was so much better it was already an effort remembering to feel grateful to *hadlam* Tapranne. Or, for that matter, to the Swami. It was not made easier by the knowledge that her recovery had pre-dated the psychic surgery. In any case it had been a hectic ten days and the children had borne it all heroically. She wondered if Zoe were up yet; that headache had made her look thoroughly rotten and underslept. Tessa had rubbed her temples with essence of palamandron flowers and done her soles with nasturtium oil.

From where she sat she could see through the Waikiki Bar's entrance to the lifts beyond. A note chimed, doors opened and Mr Mokpin stepped out hand in hand with two little Chinese girls. He was not wearing his collapsed fez today, she noticed; he was in a glossy suit and his hair looked damp and recently combed. The persona of the ethnic stallholder deep in a quarter of the Wednesday Market seemed to have been scoured off. This was a Chinese businessman approaching her with a smile of recognition and a copy of *The Times of Malomba*. At the entrance to the bar he said something to the little girls, who curtseyed before scampering off.

'Good morning, Mrs Hemony. Please forgive my lateness. I was playing with my nieces. Children, you know. One loses all sense of time.'

'Pretty little things. And such charming manners.'

'Oh yes.' Mr Mokpin quickly wearied of the topic of children. 'I see you're drinking the speciality of the house rather than *masan-masan*. A wise choice. The *masan-masan* here is terrible, not genuine at all. They try to westernise it by adding sugar and some sort of cola. A disaster, of course. Should you ever consider being my guest here for a meal, you must allow me to choose for you. They still do some genuine Hakka dishes. Although I must admit that occasionally two different cuisines can blend most happily, isn't it so? They make an excellent kittens in aspic. I believe they drown them in brandy and *mao tai* so the flavour comes from inside. But of course, I was forgetting. You are surely vegetarian.'

In his businessman's mode he was evidently a gastronome. Tessa listened to him discussing food for another five minutes, at the end of which he must have thought he'd done his bit to make up for arriving late. 'So the International Money Order is cleared?'

'Apparently.'

'Capital. Have I then your authorisation as the Swami's agent to dispatch? I will need your signature. Also of course the money, ha-ha.'

'I want to amend the order slightly,' she said, running down her own copy with a biro. 'Here, yes. I specified one hundred fifty-mil bottles of *karesh* oil. I'd like to increase that to five.'

'Five hundred?' Ong Mokpin produced a slender calculator and tilted its solar cells to the light. 'Another five hundred dollars, Mrs Hemony. At one dollar twenty-five.'

'Oh no, Mr Mokpin. You should be giving an extra discount on an even bigger bulk order.'

He glanced at her approvingly before returning to his calculator. 'One dollar seventeen. Best price. Four hundred and sixty-eight dollars. Freight and packaging will be proportionally more, naturally . . . You evidently share my confidence in *karesh* oil as a potential big seller.'

'I've begun testing its properties,' she said guardedly. 'Enough at least to justify increasing the order.' She caught his eyes on her.

'I'm delighted.'

He wanted to know why the order had to be bottled in such small quantities. Would it not be much cheaper to send a single twenty-five litre flagon? Less labour; lighter. She began explaining what he surely knew already, about shipping delays, about how essences deteriorated, about higher labour costs in the West. He watched her politely. She thought he was sounding her out; compounded weariness and boredom made it hard for her to listen to her own voice, harder still to lift the glass of punch and drag the liquid through a candy-striped plastic straw which bent at an elbow like a tiny concertina. Perhaps the full consequences of the Teacher's change of strategy were only now becoming apparent. It was surely no bad thing to have made Valcognano more productive in order that healing could be more widely disseminated. By the time she left Italy things had already assumed the proportions of a busy cottage industry: the drying and bundling of herbs, the bottling of lotions, the extraction of oils, the loading of cartons into the back of a Russian jeep which took the mule path in its primitive stride. All that was sociable and agreeable.

But this . . . She looked about her. A few Chinese noisily drinking Chivas Regal in one corner. An elderly American, possibly, with – and this was strange – two little girls eating ice cream who greatly resembled Mr Mokpin's nieces. Of course she must be mistaken. She knew it was wrong, but she was afraid the Chinese really *did* look rather alike to her. However, what was she, Tessa Hemony, doing here at ten o'clock in the morning? She didn't want this drink, she didn't want this man's company no matter how compulsive his shop. Above all she didn't want to be talking business. What did she have to do with orders and cash?

Worse still, was this to be her future? The Teacher knew he could rely on her, but surely he didn't seriously intend starting her out in her forties as a buyer? Perhaps this was only the first of many such bars she would find herself in at ten in the morning. Maybe Ong Mokpin was merely number one on a long list of men in electric blue suits with calculators. Fifteen years ago – no, less, far less – she would

161

have identified this as selling out to capitalism. By now she knew that capitalism was really only another word for making a living; but the fact of the matter was that Tessa had never actually *made* a living and had no intention of starting now.

She was wrong; of course she was wrong. The Chinese at their table laughed hysterically. A plate of what looked like fish covered in pink glue had arrived for them to pick at as they drank. She was wrong because in a moment of depression she had fallen into the error of striving and grasping. Actually she was in bliss, right here, right now. This *now* was all there was. And quite suddenly it felt like it.

❦

Earlier that morning Laki had gone out as usual for *laran* loaves, but on returning found only Mrs Hemony at the breakfast table. Zoe's absence alarmed him; he wondered how much her mother knew about last night's escapade. Rapturously treed as they had been by Father McGoohan and colleague, they had not been able to change their clothes and leave the pagoda much before two in the morning. They found the Nirvana's kitchen door locked and had been forced to go in round the front, astonishing Raju. The night porter, mildly drunk, pulled himself together enough to say, 'Good evening, miss,' in English. Laki had winked at him with the insolence of the self-pleased and Raju added in broadest Saramu dialect: 'Huh. Sweet fruit, sore belly . . . Can't see you. You're not here.'

In the light of early day as he set off for the bakery, Laki began to have doubts about old Raju. They were comrades, right enough. Fellow-exiles and all that. But even comrades had their price and he was not convinced the old man was proof against Mr Muffy. He was never going to find another job at his age. Loyalty, Laki knew, had a way of flexing under the right pressure. Maybe all along he'd been the proprietor's paid ear?

'She's got a bad headache this morning,' the missus told him in answer to his enquiry as he unloaded redundant bread on to the table. Flakes of crust stuck to his cotton uniform. A bird fluttered expectantly to the nearest chair-back. 'Also her stomach seems a bit upset.' Laki, remembering the draughts of stream water, was not surprised. 'I can't understand it, it's so unlike her. She was perfectly well last night and I'm sure we all ate the same things yesterday.'

'And the boy?'

'Oh, Jay's just lazy.' She glanced around and slipped a hand over his, drawing him closer. 'I couldn't find you last night. I wanted to give you something but you weren't there.'

'Missus, I sorry. I not knowing. I'm to playing with friend who work in bakery.' He poked at one of the loaves.

'That's all right, Lucky. Never mind. But if sometime today you'd like –'

'Trouble, Mrs Hemony?' broke in a voice and Laki snatched his hand away from under hers. Mr Muffy was advancing across the room through a cloud of finches.

'Certainly not,' Tessa said. 'Why should there be trouble? I was just thanking Lucky here for bringing our lovely bread. This young man's an investment, Mr Muffy. Hang on to him.'

'Only when we do the accounts are we knowing if an investment is a profit or a loss, madam. We shall see. At this moment I need my investment to go to Banji in order for buying more paint. If you come back next month, Mrs Hemony, you'll see a new Nirvana. We're making betterments. Throwing out the rubbish' – he shot his bell-boy a poisonous glance – 'and rating up the properties. Stocktaking. Rationalising the asset. In these days of global-wide inflation we are having to let business efficiency be our ruler, isn't it?'

Laki was sent straight off without being allowed even to do his round with the incense brazier. He took with him a long list of requirements and only enough small change for their transportation. He had to hitch a lift to Banji, taking longer than planned because the lorry driver and he stopped to watch a dogfight in one of Malomba's unofficial pits. He bet his return fare. There was a lot of blood and yelping for the best part of half an hour, and when the two bodies were dragged from the pit by a hindleg apiece only one was still twitching and it was not the one he had backed. Clearly the trip home would also have to be begged.

Once in Banji he went to the factory's trade counter and leaned heavily on it for a long, long time while indolent youths laboriously trundled the wrong drums of paint out of the recesses of a warehouse, then trundled them all the way back again. In fact it was mid-afternoon before his order had been assembled and another hour until he could arrange its carriage into Malomba. By the time he fetched up again at the hotel, dispirited and very hungry, it was almost six o'clock. Leaving the drums of paint tucked round the side he made a furtive entry through the kitchen, surprising Raju in a pre-supper snack.

'Where the hell did you get to? Muffy's been on the phone to the factory all day. They had to stop painting. Your fur's singeing, my boy. I tried to cover for you, of course.'

'Of course, uncle. Thanks.'

'All right. Oh, and that woman left this for you.' He produced a sealed packet. 'I hope it was worth it . . . They asked me to say goodbye.'

'You mean they've already *gone*?'

'Checked out this afternoon.'

Punitively, Laki declined to open the envelope then and there beneath Raju's nose. Privacy was essential. He took the back stairs two at a time and let himself into his lair.

There he ripped it open and out spilled Zoe's bracelet, a letter, and a wad of money which made him sit down. Incredulously he counted it. It seemed like five thousand. He counted it again. Suddenly it felt all wrong. Okay, he'd tried it on. Of course he had. But . . . He thought of the missus knocking on this very door two nights in succession. He thought of last night in the pagoda. Above all he thought of last night in the pagoda – *'Mister* Lucky!' – and their intimate imprisonment. That was something he never would forget. As blonde as gold; long blonde hair melted into a secret puddle beneath her own dress; later, her mouth soft on his own. Slowly he picked up the letter.

Dear, dear Lucky –

Thank you, thank you for making our (especially my!) stay in Malomba so wonderfully memorable. You are an exceptional person and I truly *know* with that sunny nature of yours you'll be as lucky as your name implies! I have the happiest and most confident feelings about your future.

Please give our very best regards to your family, especially to your mother. I'm so sorry we couldn't say goodbye properly, but we only knew we were going at the last minute. Just like us! But I absolutely had to say how grateful I am for all you did and particularly for looking after Jason. I'm afraid you've started something there – he can't stop talking about your catapult!

Anyway, hoping you can put the enclosed to good use, and only wishing it could be more,

> Gratefully,
> Your loving friends,
> The Hemonys

He put the letter down for more thorough translation later and picked up the money again. There were tears in his eyes. Five thousand? It had no meaning. More, it had no bearing on what had happened. Whatever the sum it would still be incommensurable, inapt. What *had* happened? Hadn't it been fun for them too? Five *thousand?* The bracelet blurred as he turned it in his fingers, held it to his nose. Pay-off.

Springing up he thrust letter, money and bracelet deep into the vine. What was the time? They could surely only be returning to the capital on the overnight bus which left at six-twenty. He might just . . . He locked the door and took off down the stairs. As he ·passed Raju in Reception he heard a shout from the office behind. Ignoring it, he leaped the front steps and out into the street.

Mr Muffy emerged and gazed at the bell-boy's departing figure. His face held the lines of a deep rage but there was satisfaction in his eyes. '*Right*,' he said. The porter said nothing but bowed his head. Behind him he heard his employer pick up the telephone. Raju put his chin in his cupped hands and his forefingers into his ears. He remained that way, staring at the wooden surface of the desk and listening to his own blood, for quite a while.

The stand at the bus station was empty.

'Left ten minutes ago,' said a driver laconically.

At these words Laki remembered there had been no address on the letter. He supposed they might have given one on checking in, although it would doubtless be as false as everybody else's. He might at a pinch wheedle it out of Ong Mokpin. But his heart recognised there had been no oversight. He knew if he wrote there would be no reply, could be no healing of snapped ends, no finding out whether the girl had really meant him to go to Italy. Overhead the first bats were bursting from under the shelters and whirling like smoke into the violet twilight. Lamps were being lit. The beggars and vendors were settling down, collecting their sheets of plastic and banana leaves into pitches for the night. The handfuls of hard-bitten onions were a further day shrivelled, the little cakes tough and dusty. He wandered sadly among the passengers and bus crews and peanut-sellers. He was bereft, as if the last ten days amounted to a significant part of a lifetime which had been abruptly carted away.

A bus turned into the station, one headlamp lit, the other lolling sightless like an eyeball on its wire. It was the daytime bus from the capital, evidently much delayed. He made a valiant attempt to be dutiful, pulling himself into the vehicle before it had stopped, elbowing his way against descending travellers.

'Yes sir, yes sir, what hotel you have?'

'Screw off, sonny.' The young man and his companion were trying to hitch themselves into backpacks while being jostled and pushed. They had that crumpled, sour look of those who had endured three or four breakdowns too many that day and had become costive from countless warm bottles of Bolly and Mops. 'Just ignore them, Steve. Don't give them an inch. Bastards.'

'Yes sir, what name hotel you have?'

A rucksack sewn all over with badges was shoved into his face. 'Phuket,' it read. 'Chiang Mai.' 'Puerto Galera.' 'Bali.' 'Kathmandu.' Further back in the bus he found two very old nuns with the yellowed skin of Europeans who had spent a lifetime in the tropics.

'Hotel, missus,' Laki said without much hope. 'Very good hotel. Golden Fortune, Seven Blessings all closed now. Many month all shut.'

One nun looked at the other.

'Burnt up. Finished,' Laki explained.

'I rather think, Agnes,' said the first nun in faultless dialect, 'that this boy is fibbing.'

'Both hotels seemed in perfect condition three days ago,' her companion agreed.

He gave it up, but not before all three had exchanged a small, wan smile of complicity.

Back at the hotel he found the front hall deserted. This was strange. The glass-paned door to Mr Muffy's office was shut, the lights out. Presumably gone home. He went upstairs to the roof and was about to undo the padlock on his plywood door when he found it missing. The door opened at his touch. He thought immediately of the money and went in, feeling in the usual place for matches.

'Do come in,' said a voice in the darkness.

A lighter clicked. A flame appeared before him. It grew from a plump, hairy fist and danced in two mirrorlike lenses above it. Laki jumped back, but collided with a soft belly behind him which in turn backed the door shut.

'No hurry,' said the same voice. 'We've the evening ahead of us. We were going to wait some time for you.' The flame descended to the floor where it kindled the home-made oil-lamp. A familiar orange glow filled the chamber.

There were two of them and they had already been busy with his toddy knife. His safe had been cracked. The vine was slashed and hacked to pieces. The floor was littered with leaves and flowers, slippery with squashed gourds. Tangled foliage had been wadded up into one corner. On the other side of their slotted mud wall the pigeons were silent. Maybe they had already flown up into the evening sky and were circling there in distress.

'Sit,' said the man, pointing to the floor. Laki sat against the wall, knees drawn up to chin. It seemed at first that they hadn't brought their canes, but then he saw them propped in the shadows. From his pocket the man took the bundle of money and the bracelet. Gently he slapped the wad of notes in his palm as he spoke. 'It's really a very simple matter, so listen carefully. This whole thing can be settled between us here and now, or you can make a special appearance in the marketplace tomorrow where your case would be investigated with considerable rigour. Clear so far?'

'Yes.' He barely recognised his own voice.

The man reached into the corner. 'What was that again? You said?'

'Yes.' Louder this time.

The sound of the cane came first, followed by a dense slamming across his arm and ribs. Then pain threw him sideways on to the floor.

'Yes, what?'

'Yes, sir.'

'We'll proceed. This money and this bracelet. When did you steal them?'

'I didn't, sir. Some foreigners gave me them just now.'

The cane sang again.

'It's true, sir! Mrs Hemony gave me them herself. Read the letter, sir.'

'What letter?'

'The letter in the envelope.'

'I saw no letter; did you, Putnil?'

'No letter.' They were the first words the man by the door had spoken.

'It sounds to me as if you're inventing things, boy.' Two swift cuts, one on either side of Laki's thighs, which sent him into a tight ball. From within the ball came sounds like those of a rabbit in a gin-trap. 'Let me ask you a straight question and you give me a straight answer . . . I do hope you're listening to me in there, boy?' The rabbit-noises diminished. 'Now, is it likely that a foreign lady, a tourist, would make a present of all this money, plus a valuable piece of jewellery, to a scabby little boy from the provinces such as you? A snot-nosed bell-boy? Is it plausible?'

'No, sir.' A whisper choked on tears.

'Ah, at least we agree on that, do we? So you admit you stole it all?'

'Yes, sir.'

'Well, well, Putnil. What a docile little thief we have here.' The cane descended once more, glancing off the edge of his face. 'On we go, then. It's come to our notice that you've been making forays into the next-door garden. Would you like to offer a confession about those, too?'

'Yes, sir. I was stealing toddy.'

'Putnil! Did you ever hear such a thing? I hope you realise the seriousness of this crime you're confessing to. Pointless sending out for a lawyer; there isn't one in town capable of

169

defending anything this grave. All toddy-making in this country is a Government monopoly. By infringing this you've been defrauding the legally constituted Government itself. His Majesty's Government. I'm a bit vague about the law, but don't you think this sounds perilously like high treason, Putnil?'

'Very like, I should say.'

'Very like,' echoed the interrogator. The mirror lenses gave back orange flames and a hunched form squashed against the wall whose white cotton uniform now had seepings of crimson. 'You aren't by any chance a Communist?'

'No, sir! Oh no, sir! I don't understand any of that.' And now he could see how heavier and heavier charges were massing, would always mass, like a wave system behind the mud brick walls. Worse than the pain was this despair of knowing however he answered was irrelevant. Whether he screamed, lied, begged or remained silent the waves were going to roll over him anyway.

'Of course, Putnil, we may have here one of the MNLP's juvenile recruits. Dangerous little vermin.' Again the cane. 'Boy! Listen to me! You can't faint yet. Was anyone else in this subversive toddy-plot besides you?'

'No, sir. It was all my idea. I . . . I took it for myself. I'm an addict, sir. A toddy-head.'

'Sometimes I despair,' said the man. He tucked the cane under one arm and lit a cigarette. 'What material is this on which to build the country's future? Still a child and already an accomplished thief, a defrauder of the Government and an alcoholic.'

It went on some little while.

Towards the end Putnil joined in and between them they methodically beat him unconscious. Then they left, smoking and whistling, their shoes echoing in the cement stairwell. As they went through the hotel they saw not a soul. The lights were on, the front doors open, no one was about.

It was as if everybody had suddenly decided at the same moment to slip out for a packet of cigarettes. Various priestly gongs and bells were sounding as the two men walked away, swinging their canes like walking-sticks: but for the glittering lenses, two old goats leaving their hotel for a night on the town. They went round the corner to where they had left the scarlet jeep ticking over.

❦

Night. Most of Malomba was asleep.

The merchants slept, the pavement vendors slept, the public nose-pickers slept.

Much of the priesthood slept, too, except for those whose duty it was to perform nocturnal observances or sound the watches with a variety of shawms and yodels. Towards midnight a select company of Left-Handed Shaktas arrived at the Lingasumin, each carrying a small fibre suitcase. They were met at the door of the blockhouse by temple maidens hand-picked for their unassuming ugliness and low birth. The girls were swathed from head to foot in purple muslin stuck with silver paper stars, so their plainness and inferiority would have to be inferred for the next two hours until the sacred moment of Punctual Divestiture. The copper-sheathed doors closed. Heavy bolts could be heard sinking deep into stone. Overhead the ruby phallus winked once.

There was activity, too, over at the pro-cathedral where an act of symbolic cannibalism had just been celebrated. It was an important Friday in the participants' calendar, for they were ritually grieving over a two thousand-year-old execution whose victim needed to be ingested spiritually from time to time. Eventually the last of the mourners went home. The great doors shut. Locks clicked. Overhead the

171

statue of the victim's mother blinked on and off with a faint fizzing sound.

In the depths of Chinatown a game turned into a drunken bout of Kung Fu. Several toes were broken. Soon, though, the players were snoring with their heads together on the floor among puddles of brandy and scattered mah-jongg tiles. Downstairs in restaurant kitchens fat carp and snow-white puppies slept in their tanks and cages.

The street-curs slept, the dray-nags slept. One by one the pigeons had returned to the dovecote in Laki's loft and now they too were asleep.

Mr Tominy Bundash slept, but not well. He was attending yet another Last Judgement. This god had grotesque ears and held a significant osier basket full of water on his lap from which not the least drop fell. Mr Bundash, in painful chains made of woven lightning, was in his usual rôle of respondent. He was having to give an account of his recent experience of being briefly alive.

'I liked it,' he said humbly. 'Sir.'

'Specify, that my ears and the water may hear,' said the god, twitching an ear and shifting the basket on his lap. From the water came a soft trilling sound.

'I . . . I liked the *fancy* of it all, sir. Everyone was so sure he knew what it was about but actually there was no real version at all, was there?' The trilling intensified and to his horror Mr Bundash observed a stain spreading across the robe which covered the sacred knees. He knew it was a direct consequence of what he was saying and he knew it was fatal.

'I . . . I liked the way the Rimmonites knew their reality was realer than anyone else's. As did the Shintoists and the Creationists and the followers of Dagon the Fish-God and Jesus the Carpenter. It made them happy. They all knew their version was right. Everyone was right: the healers and the gurus and the businessmen and the drug addicts and the freedom fighters and the police, down to the humblest guide in Malomba.'

172

'You, I suppose,' said the god. Water was now pouring down his robe and pooling around the holy feet. Mr Bundash, helpless in his agonising manacles, knew he had got it wrong and it was all up. He began to weep.

'I can't wipe my eyes,' he said miserably. He badly wished to wipe his eyes but the lightnings held him fast.

'Of course not. We have taken away your hands for ever.'

Looking down he discovered that his hands had indeed vanished and his arms were melting and running away. The basket on the god's lap was now one-third empty. It suddenly became very important that his legs shouldn't melt too, otherwise how was he to cross that blade-thin bridge to Paradise? He was sure he had to do that sooner or later without toppling off into the abyss, but he couldn't remember where this notion came from. And then he realised he couldn't remember who this god was, either. Now that he was finally face to face with the one true Lord of the Universe, he couldn't even recall his name. He tried hard to think. There had been a god of mercy and a god of vengeance, one of merriment and several of despair; of wine, of abstinence, of spring, of war, of peace, of love, of hate; a harvest-god and a famine-god and a hundred others besides. Which one was this? How could one tell? The ebbing water in the basket was trilling continuously now.

'You are nothing,' the god told him in a voice which filled Creation. 'You never were. And you shall be still less.'

'Oh no, please, Your Majesty,' cried Tominy Bundash, melting and hurting. 'Oh, why is all this necessary?'

The puddle on the floor around the god's throne had become a lake and turned quickly into a sea which spread on every side to limitless cerulean horizons. Its waters gave off a sound of harsh lament. From the empty osier basket came a dry, reptilian hiss. Slowly the god turned it upside down on his lap.

'Your Judgement is come,' he announced. 'It is that you will be emptied for a thousand aeons. Pray that at the end something may be found in you which is more than a matter of fancy. *Fancy*, indeed. Remove this Bundash.'

Thus Mr Bundash writhed in his sleep, pummelled senseless by deities: deities from Mesopotamia and Judaea, from Egypt and Arabia, from the Indus Valley and the Andes. Great tears rolled down his cheeks which he blew out with syllables of torment and sadness. On either side of him his wives watched in alarm.

'Oh, he suffers. It's dreadful, Laksha.'

'It's the cheese you gave him, Jineen. Always you give him cheese and always he has nightmares. Let's wake him.'

'We must be careful how we do it. When the soul's out of the body it may snap its thread and wander for ever trying to get back in.'

'You are a superstitious creature, Jineen. Sometimes I'm wondering if you're the best sort of wife for a Moslem gentleman like Tominy-*da*. I at any rate know how to do it without breaking anything,' and her hand went out full of skill and affection.

And bit by bit Mr Bundash's tears ceased and his features smoothed and at last rearranged themselves into those familiar as dutiful husband, fond father and official guide to Malomba.

Somewhere far off, meanwhile, the Hemonys were doing their best to sleep on the bus. They jolted along through the dark enjoying the tourist's feckless luxury of getting away scot-free. If so, it was their only enjoyment. Back at the bus stand in Malomba they had experienced a moment of total recall for the outward journey and opted to spend extra on a rival company's air-conditioned vehicle. It was called a HiWay Kruser and had a small lavatory at the back which particularly commended itself to Zoe. They even, for a further consideration, managed to obtain seats conveniently located at the rear.

Thirty miles into the journey it was apparent that this had been a strategic error. Because of the air-conditioning none of the windows could be opened and the refrigeration system soon broke down. The small lavatory at the back began, subtly at first and then with increasing assertiveness, to dominate the entire bus. Whenever its door was opened it exhaled ammoniac stench. Quite quickly Zoe came to hate each person who used it and began longing for a breakdown in order to escape, however briefly, into fresh air. Towards midnight her prayer was answered. The fan-belt snapped and vendors appeared from nowhere, shoving aboard with trays of oilcakes and fish sauce. The Hemonys wandered about with the other passengers in the dark, slightly stunned, kicking at loose pebbles and yawning at the thick screen of gibbet-trees on either side of the road. In a while the journey got under way again, the other passengers firmly resuming their previous seats.

Four a.m. found them in a provincial town only thirty-eight miles from the capital. There was an unaccountable change of driver and a wait of half an hour. 'Breakfast time, madams and sir,' said a man who had a seat at the front of the bus. A holy book bound in ivory had been chained to his right wrist at his coming-of-age; the silver manacle had worn thin. The Hemonys sat at a formica-topped table in a canteen ablaze with strip lighting. They stared at each other, at unwanted bottles of soft drinks and the geckos scurrying about the warped plywood ceiling. They had been decanted into an un-world on an altogether alien planet. They were mute with shock.

Once the bus had started again, the realisation of their journey's approaching end brought them slowly back to speech and consciousness.

'*Porco Dio*, what a trip,' said Jason, his eyes gummy with sleep secretions. 'I feel filthy.'

Both Tessa and Zoe were experiencing the same sensation of being thoroughly contaminated. It was not just that the breath of the lavatory had built up into a kind of sticky lacquer which seemed to coat them from hair to feet. There was the sense also of an absent grubbiness, of there being something behind them which would be less easy to think about in full daylight.

'Actually,' Tessa told Zoe after a long pause, 'I left the kid rather a lot of money.'

'Who, that bell-boy? Honestly, Mum. You're so . . . He'll only fritter it. I got to speak to him a bit, you know. I've a pretty good idea what he was like.'

'Maybe. Though you mightn't have understood his predicament, quite. He was very young and far from home, and whatever else I *am* a mother.'

'And I'm probably a better judge of character, Mum. You're bound to be a bit out of touch with people my age.'

'Perhaps,' conceded Tessa with a secret smile. 'Even so, I'm not sure it was right to leave him your bracelet. The Teacher himself gave you that.'

'I'd got sick of it, hadn't I? And the kid took a fancy to it, like I told you. I expect he'll pawn it. Come to that, I'm not sure it was right leaving him a lot of money.'

'It'll be a help,' said her mother chidingly. 'A sum like that could completely change someone's life. It'll go straight to his family, if I know him. Anyway, it's only money.'

Jason listened to this while trying out expressions of disgust in the window. 'I just wish I'd got his catapult. You two never saw it, but it was all carved with flowers and things. I think he would have given it to me. I probably knew him better than either of you. Except Mum, perhaps,' giving her a vitriolic glance.

'He was a good friend to us all,' said Tessa diplomatically.

And in this desultory fashion they bumped along without ever once mentioning their friend by the name they had believed was his.

Presently they entered the capital's sprawling outskirts. Dawn was in the air. As if by consent the whole subject of Malomba was dropped. That was yesterday, somewhere else entirely and now separated from them by a night of such unreality that a curtain – hectically embroidered with fleeting glimpses of numberless miles and hours – had dropped between *that* and *this*.

Nevertheless, each was no doubt condemned for ever to retain a private version, even one unrecognisable to the others, as if bearing away a farewell-fruit for cautious consumption over the years. Something luscious, full of the tristesse of Afterwards, which concealed a lethality all had sensed but none known how to see. *That time in Malomba.*

But now it was today. Right here, right now. It had been a successful trip: backache cured and new essences bought. Mission accomplished. Soon the bus would stop. Soon a shower and a cup of coffee.

Bliss.

Far behind in the holy city dawn was also in the air. Early rays caught the crescent moon fixed atop the Glass Minaret. Carved from a single quartz crystal, faceted and mounted in silver, it flamed and sparkled some minutes before the sun edged over the hills to light the rest of Malomba. The muezzin cleared his throat over the Tannoy system and phlegm crackled to the outskirts. At this hour there was about the Ibn Ballur mosque an austere smugness appropriate to one invariably up first, eagerly setting about the business of a new day while benighted neighbours were still sodden in sleep. Yet things were beginning to stir elsewhere. With a clap of wings the pigeons on the Nirvana's roof pulled themselves into the turquoise sky, white breasts catching fire on the eastward quadrant of their circlings. Somewhere a trumpet squealed like a rooster.

Also on the hotel roof Laki opened his eyes in a growing puddle of light beneath the hole in the ceiling of his den. He frowned. At first he thought he was paralysed but by small, willed movements found he lay securely trussed in bonds of pain. Little by little he worked some slack into these bindings, enough to raise his head an inch off the floor. Remembering everything at once from the previous night, his next thought was of being alive. Not this time, then . . . It called for an inventory. He dragged himself slowly to the dovecote wall and leaned.

It was a scene of endings, the strengthening light revealing each detail of his home's ruin. The cement floor was covered in the snot of burst gourds. Among the leaves and blooms and hacked-off stems were trampled his few clothes. Near the door lay a single cigarette end. He looked down at himself. His uniform was slashed and stiff with brown maps of blood. One hand was a shockingly inflated rubber glove, its palm purple and shiny with tightness. For the moment he didn't dare examine his other wounds, but he knew what they would be like: welts cracked partly open, lacerations, deep bruising; maybe a bone or two broken in his hand. No real damage, nothing lasting.

What was lasting lay all about him: a view of something which had come to an abrupt end a few hours ago in slime and destruction. His beautiful lair was finished for good. Whatever else, he would have to quit Malomba. The Beetles didn't warn twice. Back to Saramu to lie low for a bit and recover and then . . . Who knew? Something would turn up. He felt a sudden relief. He'd wanted a change, hadn't he? Well, he'd got one. He would never again have to appease Mr Muffy. Just go downstairs, collect his back pay, buy himself a few clothes and get on a bus. He could be home by early afternoon and not empty-handed, either; it was quite a bit he was owed. A shame about Mrs Hemony's money, of course. But it had come so arbitrarily and he'd had it for so short a time it had never really felt like his. It was an unreal sum, anyway. Things were almost cheerful after all. If only his hip wouldn't hurt so much. Slowly he reached round and from underneath him pulled his catapult. The pain eased. Good. At least he still had his *kancha*. It was as well he hadn't been able to use it. Heaven knew what they would have done if he'd produced a weapon.

Gongs from the city. Bells. An ostrich-skin drum. The familiar patter of falling drops. The water reminded him of an immense thirst. His mouth tasted of rust. A drink and a clean-up. He rolled on to his knees trailing strands of gourd mucus, and found himself looking straight into a smashed fragment of mirror. He confronted his own unlovely image. The top of one ear was torn and dried blood caked a swollen cheek. One eye was puffy, part closed. But the daylight now pouring through the hole showed him something else. It set him back on his heels in the mush, holding up the mirror and moving his head stiffly from side to side so the light could catch his face from every angle.

Gently he brought up his inflated hand and with a finger lightly touched his chin, the corners of his upper lip, his chin once more. There was no mistaking it. Old Raju had been right after all. It really could happen without warning, overnight, just like that. He had a fantasy of going out to the barber and commissioning his first shave. That would definitely be a little premature and might provoke some embarrassing joshing. Nevertheless, there was no doubt. He got painfully to his feet, went to the door and out into the brightness pouring over town. He checked in the sliver of glass again. No doubt whatever. *Ā n lil-hun.*

It hurt Laki to smile, but nothing like enough to stop him.

Downstairs in his office Mr Muffy was also making an early start, full of energy on this the first day of his new régime. He was studying a print-out with satisfaction. It proved clearly in black and white what he had suspected. If he ploughed back the salary he owed that disgraced bell-boy – who need not now be paid – he could begin rebuilding the pigeon loft on the roof. Pigeons were the thing nowadays. Chickens wanted too much room and were always getting 'flu. Pigeons looked after themselves. Only yesterday morning in the Wednesday Market he'd seen pigeon meat on sale at twenty-nine *piku* a kilo. What was more, next to baby goats pigeons were the most popular sacrificial animal. He'd heard the Vudusumin alone had a standing daily order for thirty.

Demand, supply. No economy could be entirely on the rocks while the priests drank dove blood. He tore off the paper and put the machine back in a drawer. Business efficiency. Realism. A plan. There was no arguing with that.